DORIAN

DORIAN

BY
LINDEN J. DEBIE

RESOURCE *Publications* · Eugene, Oregon

Resource Publications
An Imprint of Wipf and Stock Publishers
199 W. 8th Ave., Suite 3
Eugene, OR 97401

www.wipfandstock.com

PAPERBACK ISBN: 979-8-3852-0464-9
HARDCOVER ISBN: 979-8-3852-0465-6
EBOOK ISBN: 979-8-3852-0466-3

04/03/24

This is a work of fiction. Names, characters, places, and incidents either are the product of the author's imagination or are used fictitiously.

FOR MARY

Dorian Gray had been poisoned by a book. There were moments when he looked on evil simply as a mode through which he could realize his conception of the beautiful.

—OSCAR WILDE

Contents

1

THE SANDS HOTEL, LAS VEGAS, 2000

ORIAN Fist clutched then clicked the handheld remote
device and a woman dressed like a circus clown jumped
up and down. He had a headache, so he pushed the mute
button even before the din got out. But the noise was visible as
the screen flashed in sequence a hysterical mob jumping like the
woman, the woman still jumping and pumping and clapping
wildly, and a new car with a vamp making hugging gestures in and
out, up and down, as if she were a robotic vacuum cleaner sucking
you into the scene, sucking you into the prize that produced all the
excitement.

"Fuckin' gits, all of 'em," he sighed.

Still, he remembered with a slight sense of jealousy and a
strange but familiar tightness in his pants, his mother in sacred
trance before the glowing altar, transfixed watching game show after game show—the only time she was inattentive. That and when
she did her makeup. She got addicted to game shows when she was
herself a contestant on *Queen for a Day*—a "runner-up" but last of
three. That was back in the days of radio. Newly pregnant with a
child she would miscarry, her husband Jimmy was overseas fight-
ing at Tarawa, then Iwo Jima, then Okinawa, where a jungle rash

hospitalized him for the rest of the war and probably saved his life. She traded hard-luck stories with two other seemingly desperate housewives. In the wings awaited the peasant's throne, mantle, and scepter, tacky low-budget props that they were, and the more practical prize—usually a household appliance or a piece of urgently needed medical equipment to save a child's life. Dorian's mother, Susanna, tearfully shared her pregnant, washing machine-less, war bride story to a voting audience—likely rigged, but couldn't match the plight and desperation of Rita Bernardi, who lost her parents to the fascists and her husband at the Battle of the Bulge. Susanna later confided to Jimmy, "Rita called me a Kraut to my face. Even so," confessed Susanna, "I could only pity her, and I wanted her to win."

But Dorian, who had been brought up in a guileless world without conspiracy theories or even reasonable suspicion, knew why his mother was a contestant and why her story was lame in comparison. She wasn't there because she was hard up. "I wonder if she ever figured that out?" he pondered aloud to himself. Now in his head, "She was there because she was gorgeous, a bona fide nymph. Blond, buxom, full-lipped with a cream complexion, and legs that started way up from her shapely hips and round thighs and came down like a narrowing river, curved but perfectly symmetrical where gently at the knees and blossoming bud-like, they gave way to athletic-hard calves that adored high heels, heels bearing tiny feet—feet that ordinarily and by the practical law of bipedal locomotion are ugly. Not those feet. They defied footness and were simply lovely, which is why she didn't walk but floated." So he said.

Mute off, he clicked the remote again and a man dragged the fly-riddled, rotting corpse of his dead wife to his famine-stricken field for burial.

Click.

Now we know why she won the car. An announcer's voice, utterly artificial and laughably unconvincing, beckons us to a crowded lot filled with the very car the clown woman won. It appears that the model isn't moving. Flashing back in Dorian's imagination it was as if the game show announcer was saying, "If only you could own the car that the clown won."

"These remotes have memory if I'm not mistaken." Dorian knew all about marketing.

Click.

And so, we learn that the man's wife died from known causes. It seemed to have nothing to do with moving inventory in the auto industry. Yet Dorian couldn't shake the feeling that we know more about how the man's wife died than we do about market forces, and yet the woman died nonetheless of treatable causes.

Twenty-six years earlier at DAA Consulting and Marketing, Dorian had proved his skill in moving inventory. Thanks to his ingenuity the client automaker offered a lease deal and production couldn't keep up with demand. That was Dorian's muse, but he called it his "science." Later in perhaps his last and greatest marketing project and with the SUV fad in full swing, Dorian would convince Floridians that they needed four-wheel drive in order to keep their families safe. Flat and snowless, Floridians would buy his SUVs because he was able to prey on their fears. Dorian was a predator.

An engineer turned design and marketing expert, Dorian commanded the sizable salary that he did with this voodoo-deemed science. At DAA he had at his fingertips a room full of Apollo DN100 computers he was intimately familiar with because of his close, personal relationship with Mike Sporer and Bernie Stumpf. Thanks to them he had them configured and outfitted to his liking. All they did all day was generate statistical models. They were absolutely useless at predicting market trends—no better than Art Phillips who built Dorian's current firm, Phillips Company, from scratch. Art liked to speak of his craft in terms of intuition. No, the computers were just fast counters. Really fast! They advised Dorian that the cars were moving so slowly that his client should close a factory or two before it got expensive. Without missing a beat, he magically reduced the loss dramatically and put forward a lease deal with the speed of light—literally. Voilà, they want it now! What was red is now black.

This constituted marketing science. Nor did the computers care at all about the desolate Sahara and its problems or whether the man's wife would be missed. As lightning fast as putting together a lease scheme, they could have connected her diagnosis with a cure. But that wasn't what they were programmed to do. Neither was Dorian programmed to care. Except for one thing.

He loved it when people called him the "young wizard." But it never struck him as odd that he called himself a scientist. He was a wizard of science and in the numbness caused by what he was really passionate about, he saw no contradiction there. When he left the field of engineering to take the offer in marketing research he reflected little on the implications in terms of vocation. As distant as the idea of law is to the soulless lawyer who makes a lot of money litigating, well, since it was just another company with more money, what was there to reflect on? Nor did he reflect on the move itself—reflect no, calculate yes! That it was a company in a different place at that particular moment in time made it the right move. It fit into a disturbing pattern.

There were some early signs of that dark pattern, but nothing anyone could have anticipated. Born in 1953, Dorian's mother decided to hold him back a year although he was eligible for kindergarten at the age of five. It was the saving grace that kept him from endless juvenile teasing and combat. He was from kindergarten on the oldest in his class and the youngest looking. Had he entered public school when he could, with his baby face and small stature, he would have been trounced. To some extent, he was just a late bloomer. Susanna was by no means clever enough to have considered this to Dorian's advantage—well, to a point. Later she said that very thing, surely as an afterthought. But periodically the woman would say and do things that were so out of character, so thoughtful, that you might shake your head and wonder if you had misjudged her, that she wasn't just a pretty face. And then she would demonstrate such a lack of depth and such incredible, if sweet, naivete that every assumption got roundly reinforced. No, she wanted him home, even if it was just another year. But it was perfectly legal, and she came up with a convincing story.

So, Dorian was always the youngest in the crowd, even when he wasn't. It became necessary that be the case.

Dorian drifted away from his thoughts to listen for a moment, insouciantly dismissing the news show for "carrying on" about the tragedy unfolding in the Sahara. But he found it far more tolerable, as background noise, than the game show. After all, there was his mother to think about.

He knew she loved him in that cold way of hers—like he was an extension of her beauty, her self-image, her need to be surrounded by admirers. She dressed "my two boys" (Mark was the youngest), impeccably and to match. They weren't twins; two years apart and opposite in every way. The clothing wasn't exactly feminine, while he vaguely remembered feeling kind of sissyish in them. Rather, the wardrobe was essentially epicene and prissy to excess—like with blue bell-bottoms and little sailor hats to match the boat shoes and anchor vest. But this was way back when they were young, and only the surviving photographs confirmed his distant memory of being shown off. She didn't press it beyond reason, nor would the ex-marine Jimmy allow it for long. His boys were "men." So, when the boys became aware of the fact they were being "dressed," Jimmy but especially Mark put his foot down, and the self-indulgent fashion show ended without a quarrel.

Oddly, Dorian was far less clothes conscious than Mark. Oddly so because it was Dorian who could suddenly be overwhelmed by his appearance. Usually by a mirror, but sometimes by a comment. He habitually stared at mirrors, yet what he sought there was not his substance but his image. It was his image that obsessed him. He was so self-conscious and yet so often oblivious to his surroundings. As a result, things would sort of explode in the moment—be it in horror or in a fit of elation. The more even-keeled Mark had an organized closet and an outfit picked out for school the next day. Dorian, lethean that he could be, each morning pulled clothes out of the latest batch of laundry and wore whatever was there. Usually unmatching, occasionally with a rip in the crotch (he spent one lunch period hiding in the playground's arbor holding his butt), and always unironed.

Why did it suddenly bother him? After all, it was his fault. He could have pestered his parents as much as Mark—but it never occurred to him until now. She was so consumed with her appearance, which he conceded was dazzling—every day, every day that youthful, pretty picture, every day she at her makeup table never even watched him leave the house.

Click.

Naturally another commercial.

Ah, his latest marketing product, a magnificently engineered luxury car. Of course, nothing of that engineering was mentioned. That would be to believe the consumer was intelligent. Rather, the music swelled, and the camera narrowed to a beautiful, arid desert scene, then rocketed up as with the eye of an eagle, then shot down again at light speed to a postpile with a half-naked muscleman doing what male dancers never do, an *en pointe* pirouette, long hair flying all around and around and around. A radio voice peddled, "When you're at the top of the world you want to stay there. Even if it means, they have to come to you." A hermit-like beggar, bearded and disheveled, wild-eyed and twitching, clawed his way over the summit and handed the now stationary bodybuilder a set of keys. The screen faded, and the glistening car came into view. Someone who talks really fast said something about lease options and we're done. We never heard a word about the car or its state-of-the-art engineering.

Dorian could care less. If they sell, fine. If not with a click of his mouse, foreign markets would be flooded with them at what would still be a considerable profit. Not what he would have liked, but enough for the company to gush over the boy genius.

Suddenly apprehensive, he got up, went to the bathroom, and stared at the mirror. Dorian never passed a mirror without pausing. What was it he heard that reminded him so much of the fiasco prompting his early departure from the Pomona office? Again, aloud and yet alone, "Was it the day before yesterday?" Now only in his head, "Ya, but it was said in passing. Maybe it wasn't even meant to be overheard. They did laugh. Something about, 'Oh my God, a gray hair in Dorian's beard. Impossible! He's like Peter Pan, he'll never grow old. Ha, ha, ha.'" Aloud again, "Disturbing!" Then silently, "And there's no gray at all. Nor will there be." He picked up the razor and shaved.

By the time he got back to the room the newscast was over, and the entire world had forgotten the dead woman. A moment later they forgot the Sahara. A moment after that all they cared about were Dorian's cars. Dorian was OK with that. But what he really wanted was to remember that first date he had in high school, the one that changed his life.

2

CERRITOS, CALIFORNIA, 1971

DORIAN was cute, but he didn't really feel it or care much. A means to an end, he thought, but he was too self-conscious to try and rate himself. Eight or nine, maybe, not a ten. He was blond with white, straight teeth thanks to the braces his mother insisted on. His eyes were dark brown, and his soft looks were on the delicate side. His skin appeared soft as well, ivory in color reflecting his German heritage. However, that all changed in the summer with the California sun and the tan that came with little effort to beach lovers. Although in his youth he was always small for his age, by the time he was a senior in college he had grown to six foot two. Still appearing much younger than he was, he was tall, lean, and good-looking.

In high school girls chased him, but he was the last to know. He loved the attention when it came. It was exhilarating and made time fly—and it put him in the moment, which was where he rarely was. Designing was for him like daydreaming, and daydreaming was his forte. But he wanted sex, and he wanted it without commitment. Hell, he couldn't even talk to girls he liked or might be interested in. So shy. So insecure. But others, male and female, that great flock of people who fawned over him, well they were so much duckweed on an old farm pond. For the bit players in his personal drama, he was a veritable chatterbox. Positively charming, his wit and humor were foils disarming meaningful conversation, and it gave him the sense that he was the center of attention which was often the case. Yet in spite of resolutions to the contrary, he would occasionally be drawn into meaningful conversations. But it made him feel like one of those hapless Ice Age creatures who blindly stumbled into the nearby tar pits of La Brea. There to be stuck fast with no place to run, and an unpleasant, unwanted palaver to endure.

Dorian floored his Ford Cortina over the dead, brown grass of Ghar High School. In the summer a seasonal high-pressure ridge forms in the Pacific near the California coastline. This blocks any storms approaching the coast. Rain is rare. The ridge breaks down with the onset of cooling weather in the fall and builds up again in the spring. But the dry air and mild climate became a magnet for migrating families. From Los Angeles inland Southern California was filling up with people ever since the end of the war, people just like Dorian's parents. "War rats," the locals called them. But dead grass was better than brown snow.

Dorian grew up in Cerritos, a short fifteen miles away from Long Beach Memorial Hospital where he was born. About twenty-five miles from downtown LA, Cerritos was still sparsely populated. It had just changed its name from Dairy Valley, once considered the "Hay Capital of the World." Dairy farms were ubiquitous. In fact, when in 1967 Dairy Valley became Cerritos, there were 3,500 people and 32,000 cows. But the climate and the postwar growth soon changed the picture. New zoning regulations made life difficult for the farmers, not to mention the overnight wealth come to rubber-booted dairymen whose real estate was suddenly worth a king's ransom. Many of them moved east to dairy farms around Chino Valley in Southwestern San Bernardino County, and others headed further north to places like Ripon near Sacramento.

Dorian knew these old Dutchmen pretty well. His father had gone straight into the real estate business after the war and found out how timing and location make all the difference. Jimmy made a small fortune in the business with very little effort, and a lot of his money was made selling dairies to developers. Which is why Dorian got to know some of these heavily accented Dutch farmers. He would often joke that the old dairymen he knew from his childhood would suddenly show up at his father's office or at their home, driving a black Cadillac instead of an Oldsmobile. But in spite of their newfound wealth, they still smoked White Owl cigars. Conspicuous consumption only went so far.

Through the Cortina's dirty windshield, the spectacular Sierra Nevadas invisibly stood choking in the brown, smog haze, along with the denizens of Los Angeles County. He flipped on his car radio expecting his favorite rock and roll station, KRLA, and instead got the tail end of a news report. "Mark's been fuckin' with my radio again. He keeps it up and he's walking from now on."

The narrator was going on about the serious problem of pollution in Los Angeles. "Every child will experience the loss of half their lung capacity by the time they turn twenty." Dorian angrily punched the radio button and tuned it out. KRLA came to life, and he sang along to Jan and Dean's "Surf City." LA smog was notorious in those days, but California eventually responded with the stiffest pollution restrictions of any state. But Dorian was and always would be utterly unconcerned about the environment. He was a master at avoiding issues and sidestepping the rules, and chameleon-like he could change his complexion in a moment. Consequently, he was never identified, some fifty years later, as the primary American consultant to Volkswagen, when they were fined thirty billion dollars for rigging diesel engines to pass US emissions tests. Dorian knew how to cover his tracks. He provided the computer know-how—how it got used was their business, the backdoor out of the hardware with no trace, "fail-safe."

"Shit, no parking and late again for speech class." Dust and dry grass flew everywhere as he did a donut not to miss a small space near the south fence. He jumped out of his car not bothering to lock the door and began his one-hundred-yard dash for classroom 12. The irregularly attached buildings were unassuming and laid out like a maze of covered patios. No nonsense and no adornment. Land was affordable and abundant so there was no point in building up. Consistent with that was the cheap single-story, flat-roof design. No fear of heavy snows overburdening the cover. Snow was unheard of in Southern California. Earthquakes, yes, storms, not so much, and snow never. Likewise, the outdoor hallways were long and covered with what functioned like drab Bimini tops on leisure boats, more like umbrellas for the sun than anything else. Again, altogether practical as there was little concern for inclement weather. The idea was that students would make their way from building to building outdoors where the California sun shone most of the time. There was a cafeteria, a gym (virtually every high school had a gym), as well as a football field where the success of the team determined the prestige of the school more than the education on offer.

Although the California schools were ostensibly integrated, there were no black kids at Ghar. Rather, any overt racism was directed at the much smaller population of Mexican American students. Kids from families that had been in the area decades before anybody else, but who speciously were looked upon as outsiders. They called them "beaners" for their devotion to refried beans. Less overt was the cultural antagonism toward suburban blacks, people the kids in Cerritos rarely came in contact with and knew nothing of except for the hateful stereotypes so appealing to unguided adolescents. The issue of race was not spoken of, and so it festered in ugly teenage images and slurs based on nothing real. So, when they encountered one another at a sporting event it became symbolic warfare.

Dorian was in the stands the Friday evening Ghar played a football game against Compton High, an essentially African American school with an all-black football team. Dorian could care less about football. He was there to lust after the cheerleaders. But for the true fans, the rivalry was such that the pleasantly cool, dry air of this typical Southern California fall evening belied a tension never felt at a game before. The coronas surrounding the field lights seemed to portend a miracle about to transpire, like the star above a humble village in the shadow of Rome. The band seemed to play faster and louder, the fans appeared more edgy, and the players' white doctrinaire raised aggressions that were ramped up even higher by the "uppers" many of them were on. Unknown to the coaches was the easy access to the little, white-crossed pills that were being passed out like candy before the game. Denial ran deep in these communities, denial of their kids on drugs, denial of the racism that festered in neighborhoods in isolation from one another.

No one in the stands believed for a minute Ghar would stand a chance against Compton. Compton was twice the size of Ghar, which meant they could draw from a much larger group of athletes, and the team had proved their dominance with a perfect four and zero record. But when Ghar scored a touchdown with two minutes to play to go ahead by three points, the white crowd stood up in disbelief. For two minutes they were deathly silent. When the final whistle blew the hometown crowd roared hysterically, and the entire Ghar bleacher section rushed onto the field. It was as if their righteous little David had slain the evil giant Goliath, satisfying their provincial culture with a sense of irrational pride. Now all that was left was to cut off the giant's head with an undignified celebration. Dorian was confused by the fury.

"Screw that." Dorian rushed the field only to close in on the coeds. But later as he walked over to the gym for the after-game dance he couldn't help but ask himself, "Why was beating up on Compton any different than thrashing Artesia High like we did three weeks ago? Shit, no crazy ass hysterics there." Beyond him was the vicious expression of bogus supremacy at the outcome. "We just lined up like usual for the traditional handshaking, and we all walked off the field content to unwind at the sock hop." The ultra-naive Dorian was mystified. He would learn guile down the road.

As Dorian made his mad dash for his speech class he had no sense of place and surroundings, nor any particular sense of purpose outside of mundane obligation and immediate gratification. That went hand in hand with his characteristic disregard for his surroundings. The campus had an industrial feel to it, more suitable for making auto parts than stimulating thought. And when more space was needed but money tight, modular units were an easy fix conveniently blending in with the equally drab original. Sold to the parents and teachers as temporary, these trailer-like sheds became permanent fixtures.

The prominent flagpole out front was another universal, as well as the massive sign nearby. In the case of the host of California public schools like Ghar, there was no attempt at artistic design, just a big rectangle on slender poles. Utterly functional, the letters were black on white, block style, and simply stated the facts. "Richard Ghar High School" (Richard Ghar being the district superintendent), and below that the updatable message brief and to the point. "Student Driver Ed Sign Ups Starting Now." The only attempt at originality was a decorative G at the top of the sign for the high school's mascot, a gladiator.

As he sprinted Dorian laughed to himself, "Speech, what a joke!" Also a joke were his junior and senior years having completed his precollege courses. As a junior and senior, he took speech, creative writing, California history, algebra II, and journalism. Physical education was required every year of everyone. He kind of liked history as long as he didn't have to work too hard at it. As for creative writing, it was the latest addition to the liberal arts wave sweeping Southern California school systems. Creativity was inborn and simply needed to be unleashed. No point in learning to spell or read the works of the great authors. Same for speech class—we are all born orators with something to say. He knew them to be "blow-off" courses, especially journalism. As for math, it was his strength, and it came naturally, or at least it all simply made sense to him. He even enjoyed it. Not so with the other core requirements. He would get by by the skin of his teeth in, for example, freshman and sophomore courses such as Spanish and biology. However, his transcripts would conclude with a 4.0 grade point average during his junior and senior years, as if to show the kid had finally got his act together and demonstrated his giftedness. After all, he didn't need the extra stress, and he knew how to do just enough to succeed. With his grades and his father's money, he could go to school wherever he wanted. He was much more interested in girls. But there was the problem of his shyness.

"Late again, Dorian?" Mr. French scolded.

"Well, Mr. French, truth is I was held up."

"And what was so urgent that you fell behind?"

"No, literally held up. At PE that big-ass football player, Carson Peters, held me up, in like he wanted to prove he was a monster weight lifter, and so he cleaned and jerked me twenty times. I thought maybe he could do me oh say, five or six times but by twenty, I knew I was gonna be late." The class was in stitches.

The sullen Mr. French was not amused. "Sit down and shut up."

Dorian's early timidity toward girls made asking Lindsay Tatum out traumatic. She was attractive, petite, had his mother's figure, blonde like her, and essentially vacuous. But he wasn't interested in IQs. She could have been brilliant, and he wouldn't have cared—simply more competition. The real problem was that he felt like she was his big sister. He was a junior, she a freshman but because of his youthful appearance, he felt like she was five years older than he was. All the women close to him felt older, and that too was part of a disturbing pattern.

He was so oblivious to the practical realities around him that he didn't realize having a car made him a hot item. When he finally got up the courage to ask Lindsay out he was a senior. They dated off and on throughout that year, but it was as if they were brother and sister. The question would plague him for the rest of his life. Was he capable of love? The dull-witted Lindsay was thrilled to think he wanted to marry a virgin. How could it not bother her that he seemed so unaffectionate? Riddled with sexual desire, Dorian couldn't make a move. Rejection! Too frightening. Too risky.

Jimmy and Susanna were both raised in German-speaking homes in Carlisle, Pennsylvania, and their parents took them to the Lutheran church there. The services were still in German, and that was where the two met, dated, and vowed they would marry. However, neither resonated with the services, although they understood everything being said. The cold stiffness of Lutheran worship and seeming irrelevance put them both off. When the war came they got married and Jimmy joined the Marine Corps. He trained at Camp Pendleton near Oceanside, California. Susanna found a small apartment in Long Beach. On leave, they got to explore Southern California and fell in love with it. After the war, they decided on Cerritos.

At home, they spoke German more often than English, and yet neither of them had an accent. But they were fluent in both and as a result, so were Dorian and Mark. Little did he know his German would be of great value in his later talks with Volkswagen. And although his parents were baptized Lutheran, as were he and Mark, they attended the New Life Assembly of God Church on the corner of Norwalk and Artesia Boulevard, in Cerritos. The war had scared religion into Jimmy. Although he came through in one emotional piece, he could not fathom a God that would allow such carnage. Still, he wasn't a risk taker, and he reasoned with Pascal that betting against God was a sucker's bet.

The family drifted for years and finally found a home among the friendly Pentecostals so enthusiastic in their worship. Dorian and Mark had nothing to say about it, so they went along with their parents' demands. But when Dorian graduated from high school he vowed he would never attend church again, and it wasn't for lack of faith in its substance. Without exhibiting any theological sophistication, he simply realized he could muster up equal enthusiasm in his self-worship, and it felt just as good. Even better.

At his age he knew nothing other than his church. He realized that there were other denominations, but he had no idea why. He once asked his father why they went to New Life rather than say his friend Peter's Presbyterian church just around the corner. His dad said, "I like the people there," and that was that. The pastor did have a meeting with the youth to test the sincerity of their faith, but Dorian could give no answer. He simply asked if all churches were essentially the same. Pastor Jeffries told him no, not at all, and that the assemblies practiced glossolalia or speaking in tongues, which Dorian had simply assumed was universal among Christians. "Wrong again," replied the pastor, "and that is why they are not Christian churches. Unless you speak in tongues you cannot be filled with the Holy Spirit, which is necessary if you want to go to heaven."

"But I haven't spoken in tongues," queried Dorian.

"You will," answered the pastor.

It suddenly dawned on him that he knew several really religious folks including his parents, and they neither spoke in tongues nor did most of them attend a Pentecostal church as far as he knew. It seemed impossible that they were all going to hell simply because they didn't speak in tongues and he with them. No, he would break away from that scene first chance he got.

Dorian graduated high school in 1971, dumped Lindsay, and chose an engineering school, California State Polytechnic College, Kellogg Unit. Soon the Engineering Division became the School of Engineering, and in 1972 the school changed its name to California State Polytechnic University, Pomona, the best in the state and close to home. The glass and modular architecture were functional and not particularly attractive. Still, the setting among the foothills of Southern California, essentially a coastal desert, was stunning. Warm and dry, the palm trees gave it an exotic, tropical feel for anyone not jaded by being born there, which was most people. He got in without a problem and insisted on living on campus, even though the commute would have been a short one. He stayed with his strengths, math and science, but out of an itch he couldn't seem to scratch, he was lured into a course in philosophy. He immediately latched onto the American pragmatists, scoffing at the German idealists and romantically venerating Greece and his favorite, Socrates. But it was less than a hobby, and he reasoned it was all pretty pointless. He had bigger fish to fry.

He met a UCLA coed a year younger but in the same grade and moved in with her. Her apartment was blocks away from UCLA's main campus, but his commute to Pomona was only twenty-five miles, which in those days he could do in thirty or forty minutes. The curriculum was geared toward his talents, so he breezed through college. Still, he had to endure the humanities and cover the core requirements. But his father's allowance meant he could afford tutors who made the work easy. He graduated third in his class.

Stacy O'Neal was a Scots-Irish blond with a beautiful body, quite attractive with lots of makeup, which he loved. She wore her hair long and had just a hint of the weekend hippy in her. Her style was towards the cutesy or frilly. Not necessarily expensive, but generally sexy and always matching in every respect, from the shoes to the earrings. She was warm and sweet, and she loved Dorian with all her heart. They met near the pier at Redondo Beach, both of them surfers. Even in her wet suit, Dorian could tell she had a fabulous body, and she loved surfing as much as he did. She liked it that he was athletic, that he worked out at a fitness center nearly every day, and that keeping in shape was a priority for him. She had the same ethic. They also had a mutual fondness for the outdoors, which for the time being kept Dorian in California although his growing obsession would make just about everything else play second fiddle.

Once in a while, he would meet Stacy at the UCLA commons for lunch. On a beautiful spring day in 1972, a large campus demonstration was held protesting the incarceration of former UCLA acting assistant professor of philosophy, Angela Davis. She was a member of the Black Panther Party and implicated in a violent act of retribution for which she was jailed.

Davis had studied under Marcuse at the Frankfurt School in Germany and became a communist, publicly declaring that capitalism was disastrous to human well-being. She gave several lectures on the subject essentially targeting Western colonialism and its putative commodification of people, goods, ideas, etc. into objects of exchange. She also argued against Western social conventions that she believed destroyed authentic human freedom. These conclusions were the stock in trade of Frankfurt. But growing in importance for her was the blight of racism whose suffocating influence had shaped her radicalism. Increasingly she turned her attention to the problem of racism and sexism in America. And while she remained in sympathy with communism's exposure of social inequality and abuse of power, along with their openness to the leadership of women in the party, she became critical of their general disregard of racism as a central issue. She also came to conclude with the postmodern critique that Frankfurt's rationalism was unsustainable. That critique proved to be Frankfurt's downfall. The emerging view was that the failure of Adorno, Horkheimer, Marcuse, and the rest of this loose school was their self-defeating foundationalism. Dorian would follow these developments in philosophy although unwittingly.

The time around the UCLA demonstration was pivotal in US history. It coincided with the Vietnam War, certainly America's greatest political watershed of the middle twentieth century. Stacy, curious and a bit amused by all the chanting, wanted to get up close and hear what was being said. Dorian wanted no part of it, and so he took a seat on a bench a distance from the maddened crowd. Next to him was by all appearances a UCLA professor, properly imaged with long hair and unkempt beard. He wore a button-down shirt and plaid jacket with a plastic pen holder in his vest pocket filled with pens and pencils. Dorian ignored him and focused on the coeds passing by giving each one a rating.

"This is it now," ventured the man on the bench. "No doubt about it. Vietnam marked the turning point, but this is another defining moment in American history. The country is completing its swing left. I saw it coming on since the fifties. What we're seeing here from the university chairs is a seismic shift from a population at home with essentially conservative values and almost blind acceptance of political leadership to a general distrust of these institutions. This will only intensify."

Dorian was neither patriotic nor was he the least bit interested in the morality of the war. He thanked his luck alone that he had escaped the draft by having a student deferment, along with a high lottery number if this thing were to drag on. He had zero interest in the monologue occurring next to him, and he was relieved when Stacy came bounding up to him. He left never acknowledging the stranger's presence.

3

Pomona, California, 1974

ORIAN was hired straight out of college in 1974 by DAA Engineering and Design Inc. Immediately he applied his computer savvy which in most ways was self-taught, in the development of the gull-wing technology which the company sold to DeLorean for several million dollars. It made him a celebrity at DAA, launching him into the spotlight he adored. It was here that the moniker "the young wizard" was first applied.

Stacy and Dorian got married at the stunning Wayside Chapel in Laguna Nigel spectacularly nestled amidst the palatial seaside cliffs of Southern California. Wayside remains a wedding destination magnate, and the congregation subsidizes their generous staff salaries and mission programs by hosting ceremonies, as many as three or four in a week. The hefty fee of $2000 didn't deter couples smitten by the gorgeous ocean views visible through a transparent glass and stone structure. The sensational pipe organ was built by the renowned Schoenstein & Co., with an out-of-this-world resonance that you felt as much as heard. When the organ reached its full volume the glass structure reverberated as if caught up in a roll of thunder. The high altar was stunningly sunlit and seemed perched above the ocean like a swallow's nest, allowing the congregation an inspiring view of the Pacific. The breathtaking surrounding hills created an amphitheater effect that made the whole experience surreal. Stacy insisted on a church wedding with a pastor. Dorian's compensation was that only a few friends and family were invited. Jimmy broke with tradition knowing Stacy's parents were of modest means and threw the reception at the newly opened Surf and Sand Resort in Laguna Beach with its equally spectacular views and award-winning food.

Dorian was already an up-and-coming at DAA, and Stacy got a position teaching physical education at Pomona High. They had two daughters, Susanna and Leslie Ann. The girls were adorable and had a striking resemblance to Dorian. Stacy stayed home with them planning on returning to work when the girls were a little older.

They bought a fashionable ranch-style house in Diamond Bar ten minutes from Pomona and seemed destined for bourgeois domestic tranquility. The pious Stacy insisted they join a nearby Baptist church, the church of her youth, convincing Dorian that the girls needed to grow up in the Christian faith if he expected them to be decent and moral. And when Dorian said he had vowed never to go to church again, she said it was his duty as their father to bring them up in a Christian home. So, reluctantly he acquiesced and sat patiently in the pew Sunday after Sunday hearing almost nothing that the preacher said, his mind forever drifting over algorithms, designs, and ideas of a more philosophical nature. Religion was one thing, science and philosophy were another. "Why give away your brain?" he resolved. "At least Socrates was willing to keep an open mind."

He was called out on that one Sunday afternoon when a church member, a busybody, pushy kind of man approached him at their coffee hour after the service. He was olive-complected with a tiny goatee. His lips were thin and turned up grinning in an unnatural way. He had an air of aloof intelligence about him but also pride. He said he had watched Dorian over the few short years and "noticed that he didn't notice."

"What are you saying?" Dorian stared menacingly at him.

Unfazed the man replied, "Only that you appear to be here, but you are not. You are physically here, but spiritually you are absent."

"I've got to take the girls to their ballet lesson, and I can't really talk right now," Dorian said matter-of-factly.

"Then when? Next Sunday, lunch, dinner at my house? When, where?"

"When what?"

"When are we going to have this conversation?"

"Ok, wait a second. Stacy, can you take the girls to ballet and come back and pick me up? Mister, what was it you said your name was?"

"I didn't. Darius Mifty," the dark-haired Baptist intruder replied.

"While I chat with Mr. Mifty here," he called back to Stacy. "It won't be long."

"Longer than you think," whispered Mifty.

"What did you say?" asked Dorian.

"Nothing," audible now, Mifty answered.

"OK, what's up?" said Dorian. "And by the way that name, Darius, I know it. He was a Persian philosopher, no ruler I think. Like from Iran?"

"I guess you could say it has Persian roots. But I come from nowhere especially, and everywhere essentially. In other words, I and my family have been around."

"So then what ya got for me? Hey, are you selling something? I've got all the life insurance my family needs."

"No, I'm here as a Baptist parishioner like yourself. And I see you in church each Sunday, but I can tell you are not a Baptist, nor maybe even a believer, but perhaps you are a philosopher?"

"You can tell all that, by what, my body language?"

"Perhaps."

"Well, I am a philosopher of sorts. I mean a free thinker, but my motives for being here are my own."

"You are here for your family, obviously and quite nobly so. But have you picked up anything said here at all?"

He was intrusive, to say the least. "What was his game?" Dorian silently wondered. Still, when he wasn't distracted Dorian could be lured into a gambit. "Well, I'm not entirely asleep. Let me see. Hey, why do you want to know?"

"Well, like you, I am a philosopher, a seeker of truth like Socrates whom you admire, I'm sure. But I am also a faithful Baptist, deeply desirous of bringing you to faith. So, what is it you have learned and know for sure?"

"Well, I know only one thing for sure. I want to live forever." At this Dorian couldn't contain himself and laughed out loud. All around him, the faithful stared because they had never seen any sign of emotion in the young man, not ever.

Darius beamed, "Perfect then the Baptist faith is for you."

"But I don't want to live forever on some heavenly cloud, by and by, up in the sky."

"So, you have been listening."

"I'm talking about seeing to it that what time I have lasts as long as possible."

"Well, I'm sure you will do all in your power to make that possible."

"You bet I will."

"Excellent then. You see, you have already made the first step in becoming a good Baptist. You are focused on your personal salvation. That's what we Baptists are all about. But now I'm talking about eternity. Salvation in this life and the next. We Baptists have escaped the superstitions, papism, and irrationalism of the old Catholic order. We have been freed to read the Bible and make our own interpretation—just the way you are doing."

"But I don't read the Bible."

"Yes you do, every Sunday you sit there and hear it read aloud and explained. Consciously or unconsciously the offer is there, and so like these good folks all around you, you make up your own mind. Except these exceptionally good folks don't really make up their own minds. They make up their minds to fall in with the preacher and his Baptist colleagues. Although they are being taught to see things as they are and as clearly evident in Scripture unadulterated as the Catholics do not. they will of themselves come to the correct interpretation, as long as it is consistent with Baptist teaching. But some of them will turn renegade and will indeed think for themselves, however misguided. And they will come to all kinds of creative mischief. Don't you see that is why there are so many Baptist sects, and that we have spun off a fabulous number of dissenters many of whom started their own church? In a sense, we are a greater engine of common free-thinking than the Renaissance ever was. At every turn of the road attempts at mind-enslaving unity as we see in the ecumenical movement are thwarted by our devoted followers who are bold proselytizers and uninhibited nationalists. Our Baptist lay leaders, like my protégé John D. Rockefeller, are often the richest, smartest, and most ambitious businessmen on the planet. They have found in the gospel of freedom a way by which they can be adept entrepreneurs. And I think you would fit right in if only you would come on board."

Dorian balked. "Rockefeller, he's been dead since . . ."

"A slip of the tongue," intercepted Mifty, "I meant to say my inspiration."

"But you never mentioned Jesus. Did he inspire you?"

"In a manner of speaking. Of course, it's all part of the picture. We call it freedom in Christ. We've led the way in the modern-day evangelical revolution, and soon church itself will be redundant or at least merely a source for the creative spiritual networking we desire. You might call these churches of the future, heaven's terminals."

"But what does that have to do with Jesus? Listen I need to get clear on this. Do you believe *in* this guy Jesus, that he was God, that he was born in a stable with cows and sheep and camels, and that he died but came back to life?"

"Of course, I do because it's all true."

"So, you're what they call a born-again believer?"

"Not in so many words. Let's just say I believe it happened pretty much as the Bible says. But I'm much more interested in salvation, particularly your salvation Dorian."

"Well, I'm not the least bit interested in salvation—period."

"Hey Stacy, OK kid, I'm through here. Mif ole boy—see you next week, and maybe we can talk about my new design in advanced four-wheel drive technology. Take care."

"Weirdo," Dorian thought. He was unimpressed and yet provoked. Usually, he had no regard whatsoever for anyone who wasn't offering a practical way for him to get ahead or telling him what a young genius he was. This was different and Dorian was curious, merely curious. Still, he was determined to avoid any more of this kind of conversation—not unless he could control the narrative. He wanted to focus on the relativity of truth, something he believed the best philosophers stood for. Morality would fall into the same bag. This would suit him as a way to ease his conscience for behavior the Pharisees around him might condemn.

"Pharisees," now out loud as he slammed the car door. Yes, that was a term he did pick up in church. They were all Pharisees, those who might condemn him for following his heart.

Stacy was rattling on about the girls' brilliance at ballet. Dorian knew they could barely walk. "Hell, they are two and four," he thought to himself. But to Stacy, he kept repeating, "For sure. I'm sure about that. I know this." He was reviewing his conversation with Mifty. He resolved he would never again be caught out on the defensive, and he was determined he would read more philosophy, as much as he had time for.

To Stacy, Dorian looked to be so utterly paternal as he seemed to agree with everything she said. And so, she simply overlooked several of his idiosyncrasies, like the utter distance he exhibited while the conversation with Mifty spun around in his head, like his infatuation with mirrors, like his essentially callous disregard for people not in their circle, and most odd, like his strangely uncharacteristic gullibility at the hands of flatterers. How could someone seemingly so self-confident be so insecure? Such that his gullibility could go both ways. Here was something she was not aware of, and that was that his radar was always scanning for comments about his age. Every remark was duly noted, recording with precision the frequent quips of his youthful appearance. "You're much too young to be so gifted and successful." "What are you doing in this stuffy office surrounded by all these old men?" "Young, brilliant, and good-looking, how much can one man have?" But every once in a while his radar would pick up a different signal. Toward the end of the decade, DAA was hiring a new lineup of young professionals. It was about that time that alarm over that lineup led Doran to a kind of insanity. It was 1985 and he was thirty-three.

Their circle of friends was small but fairly tight. It was utterly determined by the social life of Susanna and Leslie Ann, or the DAA professionals meeting Dorian's standards. If they passed Dorian's tolerance test they were in. Initially they naturally tended to be the same age as Dorian and Stacy, young, well-healed, reasonably laid back, and unconcerned about politics.

It was a Friday night birthday party at the home of one of Susanna's school friends. A parent, Milo Fielding, was talking and running through the sports scores. Fielding was a great salesman and Dorian admired his success, but he couldn't relate to his interests, sports, gambling, and flirting with married women. He was by no means good at any of them, which made him innocuous and acceptable. It was background noise for another boring, child-centered gathering of contemptible friends, each of whom could be dismissed with a wave of Dorian's hand. Fielding was now venturing into power hitters, his putative forte. "Barry Bonds, oh no, the Babe—wait Roger Maris."

"Power," now that's a subject of interest. It was an unfamiliar voice, but a strangely reminiscent face. A diminutive man with a mustache pushed his way into the conversation.

"Power. It does indeed come down to power. In all matters, sports or otherwise. Power, the ability to control. So clearly exposed by a subject of mine, a French philosopher of some renown, Michael Foucault by name. Power. Yes, indeed, for Foucault it all comes down to power. But not power as you might think of it. Not bad power, but the necessary way that relationships unfold."

His abrupt manner and staccato made it hard to stop him. "Take the term 'power hitters' as our friend here said. It simply means to hit a ball a long way and perhaps fairly often. Power is defined in a purely physical sense. But more subtly power is the force that propels the ball—it defines its trajectory. In that sense, we are all power hitters, whether we know it or not because we all exercise power over one another, especially sexually."

Fielding's mouth had seized up and required lubricant. All he could manage to utter was "parched," and like the flighty bird he was, he took wing. Dorian wanted to go with him, but he couldn't help being intrigued by what must be a parent, but one he had never met. Unusual, as the circle was tight and suspicious of outsiders.

"So, I didn't catch your name," Dorian's wary lips were so tight they never moved as to appear the ventriloquist.

"William Frederick Zagros," the aggressor pronounced wide-mouthed, punching out the syllables with a steady cadence. More sonorously now he lied, "The rosy-cheeked little boy talking to the birthday girl is mine."

"Hmmm, we're a kinda tight group here, and hardly ever is there someone new at our parties."

Lying again Zagros replied, "That's because I'm the uncle of the birthday girl, and we're only in town for the weekend. She insisted that my son, Andreas, be invited."

"OK, so what do you mean everything comes down to power?" Dorian was reluctantly drawn into Zagros's web.

"Well, Foucault was perhaps the first philosopher to recognize that truth was determined by power structures and their relation to sex. I mean he realized the real nature of sex. He looked way back at Greek culture and realized it was bisexual. Males had sex with males all the time. Boys with men. They played their various parts in the drama of sex and power. Tutelage for favors rendered. Socrates was notorious!"

The mention of Socrates in that context infuriated Dorian. "Get to your point," he growled.

"Right. Beyond a large body of historical and political work, Foucault managed to further the idea that truth is a human construct governed by certain biological and sociological principles."

Dorian suddenly realized he liked the guy in spite of his obnoxious manner. "You mean this Foucault fellow proved that power is OK?"

"It's not that simple. Let's just say he recognized how natural, indeed how necessary power was for human interaction. I guess you could say you need to recognize the absolute episteme of your subjectivity and embrace your power. That is the fact that you are defined by your social context, and it is a web of power plays all colliding and coalescing."

Dorian demurred. "The little I know of Foucault was that he was against all tyrannies, all abuses of power."

"Correct. His approach was primarily therapeutic. Liberation from fear. But there was nothing outside of the mix that should encourage or even demand that, no divine that required justice for all, merely that the liberation of the subject was desirable."

"Like no Ten Commandments?"

"Pure rubbish," Zagros was animated now. "Render to Caesar as little as you can, and nothing to that which does not exist. Mr. Fist," queried Zagros, "I take it you consider yourself a self-sufficient man?'

"Yes," Dorian never doubted it.

"You are your own boss, master of your destiny. So, why be shackled with powerlessness or the fear, the baggage, of an ancient ghost, a phantom soul, the perversions of the micromechanics of power producing an endless cycle of anxiety and self-recrimination? It's time for men and women to call the kettle black and be liberated from divine oppression, the stories that both created the soul and enslaved it. Our society is rotten to the core. It is a disciplinary society controlled by a narrative of so-called liberal individualism which has created the present climate of racism, sexism, and consumerism. Nevertheless, the solution is not to be found in myths and fairy tales. Knowledge, certainty, is bequeathed to the cultures of rationality, those that avoid the reasonless or the so-called suprarational explanations, and commit themselves to practical and theoretical values experimentally derived and tested."

Dorian took an extra long pull on his Martini, and suddenly Zagros reminded him of somebody he'd been avoiding. Mifty!

"Impossible," he whispered. "How?"

"How what?" asked Zagros.

"Nothing." Dorian drained his Martini and insisted he "needed" another.

Fielding glided in laughing. "Long day, Dorian? You look tired. You know that job of yours has produced some wrinkles. It's all inevitable though. We boomers are getting up there."

Zagros smiled at Dorian in a sinister way. As Dorian sped to the bar he experienced a knee-jerk reaction that felt like he had been kicked in the stomach. He stumbled, grabbed his drink, and went to the bathroom. The olives with their bright red pimentos bobbing up and down shown like warning lights on an ambulance. Sirens going off in his head, he turned on the light and stared at the bathroom mirror. His complexion was pale and his eyes wide. "What had Fielding said?" he asked himself. "Getting up there." Now thinking back, what was it that had been bothering him so much at the office lately? "Oh, of course," he remembered now, "the new young cadre of workers."

His complexion returned to normal as a plan slowly formed in his mind. He smiled and combed his hair. He splashed some cold water on his face, dried himself, and peered back into the mirror. He reached into his coat pocket and removed the ad he had pulled from the computer printer earlier that day. An automotive marketing and consulting firm, Phillips Company, in Des Moines, Iowa, was looking for a design and marketing person with an engineering background.

On the drive home, Dorian was as much himself as ever. Stacy never suspected that her husband had set off on a path he felt destined for. The next morning, he put his plan into action. He went into his office at DAA, locked the door, and began hacking the systems he needed to. For years Dorian had experimented with various hacking techniques believing that they might come in handy. In fact, he enjoyed the feeling of power it gave him along with the sense of clandestine invincibility. In time he mastered his own technique and could be considered one of the best in the shadowy field. He believed his greatest hacking triumph was an inconspicuous virus he called Little Ghost. He installed it on the computers of the IRS. Its genius was that it only appeared when the name Dorian Fist came up. At that moment the ghost would appear, literally consume any data on the subject, and disappear, not to reveal itself again until Dorian's name reappeared. He never paid a dime of federal taxes since then.

Hacks complete, there was no Dorian Fist born in 1953 at Long Beach Memorial. Nor did a Dorian Fist graduate from any California school or ever reside in the state. Never had he held a California driver's license. For the time being there was no such person as Dorian Fist. He had made the necessary connections and payments wherever a paper trail rather than a computer trail could be followed. He packed a small suitcase, transferred funds, purchased a one-way ticket to Des Moines under a false name and ID, and caught the afternoon flight out of LAX. He was gone with no trace.

Stacy came home as usual and asked the girls where Daddy was. "No clue, haven't seen him all day." She called the office but got the answering service instead. Frantic now she was awake all night. She tried to compose herself while she put the girls to bed, but it was all she could do not to burst into tears.

"Where's Daddy?" Susanna implored.

"Oh, he probably got tied up with some office matter," Stacy lied.

"But why didn't he call?"

"I don't know. I don't know."

First thing in the morning Stacy called Dorian's office and was told he left the office yesterday afternoon, and that he hadn't been seen since. After taking the girls to school she called Dorian's brother, Mark. Nothing. She then called his mom, Susanna. They managed to make each other hysterical and following that insane conversation, they called everybody they knew. Nobody knew a thing. Finally, she tried Missing Persons and got nowhere. When Stacy finally put the phone down she let out an earth-shattering scream, one that went on and on and on until breathless she fell to the floor crying and shaking.

"What can I do, where should I turn?" She prayed and prayed and cried and when she picked the girls up from school she put on a brave face although her eyes were swollen red from grief, uncertainty, and misery. She couldn't think. Days passed and then weeks and then years, and while she came to grips with the fact that her husband was gone, she slipped into a painful depression, one she struggled with for the rest of her life.

Dorian's daughter Susanna took it harder than Leslie Ann, who was so young. She adored her father, and his disappearance made her unbearable teenage years impossible to navigate through. She committed suicide in her freshman year of college. Instead of a suicide note, she left a short poem.

> I was lost to myself when the ocean swept the sand
> When faces stopped looking
> When the tide covered the shore
> And nothing was
> Nor could be
> What am I without thou?

Stacy screamed that same scream she wailed years ago, and it left her equally breathless but now her emptiness was replaced by a tumorous pain that sent her deep into a well of darkness. She only managed. Until she died, she only managed.

Dorian's parents were devastated. Susanna strangely blamed Jimmy and turned cold to him and to the world. Thoughts of guilt for nothing she could have possibly controlled ate at her, especially at night, and insomnia set in. She became reclusive, and when her hip replacement surgery went awry she complained monotonously of constant pain driving even her loved ones away. Eventually, she was bedridden and at seventy died in her sleep of a heart attack. Jimmy spent a few years trying to find his missing son, but the trail had been erased, and he finally gave up.

The DAA office experienced a seismic shock that slowly gave way to an unspoken level of mistrust among the workers. The very same experience was felt by the small circle of friends, some of the older ones being DAA employees. The unexpressed feeling was that if one of them could not be trusted, none of them could be trusted. Morale was dismal but in time and with a lot of turnovers, the incident was forgotten and the world of DAA moved on.

4

DES MOINES, IOWA, 1985

A R T Phillips was a personal success story. Born in a tough Harlem neighborhood, his mom and dad sheltered him, encouraged him, and saw that he steered clear of trouble. They both took two jobs and thanks to Art's amazing grandmother who lived with them and nurtured Art with black history and pride, Art went to Howard University filled with his grandmother's sense of enthusiasm for his people's cultural heritage. He graduated top of his class. He took a master's degree in engineering from Brown University School of Engineering in Rhode Island. He learned of a small struggling company in Des Moines, Iowa, that could be acquired for a song. He raised the money and renamed it Phillips Company. With intelligence, hard work, and determination, he built the company almost from the ground up and made it one of the industry's leaders. The first thing he did, having made his first million, was to buy his parents a house next to his in a beautiful Des Moines suburb.

Dorian aced his interview with Phillips, and Art wanted to hire him on the spot pending his references checked out. Dorian had created a new identity for himself by hacking the computers that he needed to such that his birth and education were duly recorded, his work record stellar, and it all took place in Iowa. He had figured out a way of creating a brilliant resume with an impressive list of educational and professional references all of which would be answered by him. He was a local boy now, born and raised in Iowa. Parents dead, no relatives. Single and a workaholic who never took vacations because of his work ethic. Or so it appeared. But Dorian insisted on one condition. He asked for a tour of the office, saying he wanted to get a "feel" of the people and the place. Art was glad to show him around. Of course, the motive was more duplicitous than Dorian let on. From the brief bit of research he had done, he had the sense that the office was staffed by a relatively older group of people. Sure enough, after an hour of glad-handing Dorian was satisfied and signed the contract, agreeing he would start the following Monday. He spent the Friday and the weekend looking for a home. He had callously drained most of the family's savings, transferring the money to a Swiss bank and then moving it to Iowa-Des Moines National Bank. Dorian Fist existed again, but with no traceable connection to his former self.

The buzz around the office was that Art had hired a brilliant, young computer guru with an engineering and marketing background, and there was more than a little truth to that. Under Dorian's deft hand, the business boomed, and the moniker "young wizard" resurfaced to Dorian's delight. His interview tour of the office had proven his suspicion: the staff was generally about a decade older or more than the now thirty-three-year-old wizard.

The detachment that marked Dorian's life was evident in his choice of Iowa. Iowa couldn't be further from California in every respect. But he was unconcerned about that. He measured quality of life in a different way, having little to do with geography or relationships or sense of place. Success would be determined by his sense of ego. What was it Zagros said? "Recognize the absolute episteme of your subjectivity, and embrace your power." On the plane, he looked into the unfamiliar word "episteme." It was the key to validating what one knows. What he could make of it was that right and wrong should be measured in terms of personal outcomes. One is right, that is one knows when one is personally successful at fulfilling what comes naturally. After all, what madness is there in trying to satisfy people when you can't possibly know what it is that they really want from you? No, his life would be measured in terms of how he felt, and he felt good when he felt young and successful. That had little to do with location, as long as he was able to control the social setting.

His first weekend was spent house hunting, and it took him well beyond the Des Moines city limits. He would likely live in the city or a suburb, but he wanted to get a feel for the state. Immediately he found himself among cornfields, miles and endless miles of cornfields and pig farms. The smell was pervasive and dreadful. Go into a café for lunch, it still smelled "swiney." He couldn't come up with a better term. No matter where you went outside of the city the ghastly smell permeated the air.

The land was made flat by ancient glaciers creating the perfect conditions for farming and raising livestock. Churches were equally prevalent as were small towns, like Prairie City, Monroe, Summit, and the Dutch settlement of Pella. He drove as far as Pella and stumbled on their annual Tulip Festival. He had never seen so many white people in one place, most of whom were blond. They had dressed the kids in Dutch costumes complete with wooden shoes, and there they were in regalia, clomping in rhythmic dance down Main Street, making the distinct noise that wooden shoes on asphalt make. Tulip blossoms decked the square with its faux windmill and displayed their red, yellow, and orange adornment throughout the town. He was so fascinated he watched all day and managed to find boarding. "You're in luck, every room in the town is taken but this one," he was congratulated by the desk clerk. "It was a cancelation five minutes ago. I guess you were meant to be here."

After the festivities, Dorian had dinner, went to his room, and penned the responses of his references he would type and fax the next day. He was a stellar professional, dedicated to his job, kept out of trouble, and a great team player. He was hoping to get a drink at a bar before bed. It was only about 9 p.m., but to his astonishment the streets were empty. It was as if the rapture had taken place, and all those dancing Dutch Protestants had been transported to heaven. Or as if the population had been eradicated in a biological disaster. There was nobody. Literally nobody. He stumbled into one of the few bars. Things appeared fairly normal, except the dark quarters were hardly warm and welcoming like a pub should be. Likewise, the music was too quiet for a tavern. The patrons were at small tables or at the bar, where they were being served by a female bartender who stood out as an antonym of Pella, both in manner and personified. "Hella," he silently dubbed her. The patrons seemed huddled over as if in hiding or contemplating conspiracy. They had the look of knowing they should not be here, and that their presence would be discouraged by the townspeople.

Hesitantly he went to the bar and addressed the mixologist. Hella was as pale as the morning clouds, clouds whose dark linings threatened a storm, where angry tattoos turned white into black. Blonde hair competed for attention with splenetically dyed red streaks, tossed beehive fashion, and doing an off and on, up and down, uncontrollably directing Dorian's eyes, from hair to bright red lips and back to hair. Dizzy, he needed to steady his gaze. She came around the craggy bar to wait on a table. He noticed a black widow spider tattoo where her neck gave way to her back. A tight black miniskirt encircled black net stockings trailing down to more red, these high heels with sequence.

As she returned to the bar Dorian made his first hesitant attempt at attracting the attention of the phlegmatic young woman. Silently cautioning himself he warned, "I'm on foreign soil here. I shouldn't do this." But Dorian could never resist the temptation to stand out. He looked up at her from the barstool and said, "I guess wooden shoes don't come in red?" She stared blankly at him saying nothing. He ordered his favorite scotch, a single malt, "Lagavulin, on the rocks, please." The antonym continued her blank stare.

Dorian offered to help. "It's a scotch, really peaty and smoky. Sixteen years old. From the Isle of Islay." Did he really think she would be impressed by his knowledge of the Inner Hebrides?

"If you want scotch all I have is Red Label."

Dorian was playing the foolhardy adventurer. "Red as in your lips?"

"No, Red as in my boyfriend's nickname. He's over there. The tall, big guy with the pool cue in his hands." Dorian laughed his fake laugh and followed her chin's upward motion toward the back of the bar. Nobody was paying attention. Dorian breathed a sigh of relief.

She measured a single jigger, loaded a whisky tumbler with ice, and upended the shot glass over the ice. It was so far from his California pours that even a double would have left him dry. The whole experience unnerved him. It was as if the outcasts of the community were quarantined in this dark and dingy cell née bar to do penance; that they were kept off the streets to avoid contagion, so that by morning when the good people of Pella went about their business, they would avoid any contamination from this godless underworld.

Hella wiped the bar with her towel and leaned in showing just enough cleavage to distract him. "Do you know why they call some women black widows?" she asked.

"Ya, I think so. Isn't it because they are venomous?" he chuckled nervously.

"No," she banefully smiled. "It's because after sex the female eats the male."

He threw back his scotch in one small gulp, paid his tab, and slinked back to his room. He went straight to bed. That night he decided he would hire a realtor to find him a house in a suburb of the city.

On Monday he was on the job as promised. He immediately sensed his celebrity status, and the looks of admiration or jealousy resonated with him. He was at home. He threw himself into his work. His first concept to design was an advanced airbag system. Dorian concluded that the market would increasingly look to safety, especially after what had happened with the seat belt revolution. Similarly, the marketing of airbags was initially met with a lot of resistance. Both the Ford and GM lobbies fought it tooth and nail. But Dorian saw the handwriting on the wall, and he managed to convince a skeptical Art Phillips. His design became an industry standard, and in 1984 Ford started including them as an option. It made Art a richer man than he ever dreamed. But Dorian's biggest accomplishment was also based on his prescience. He knew the industry needed to downsize if it was to survive. He convinced Lincoln and together they came up with the Lincoln Town Car, a big hit developed on the tried-and-true Panther Platform with a 5.0 V8 engine.

Dorian felt ageless as he strode the halls of Phillips Company. He met a vivacious older woman, Kimsy Clark, a forty-two-year-old lawyer in their legal department, and having gotten over his adolescent fear of girls he asked her out. She was flattered and said just the right thing. "What are you kidding? You look fresh out of college. Listen, pal, I've got baggage. I'm still settling my second divorce, I've got three kids, a dog, and a mortgage. And I'm not up to any more wear and tear."

"Whoa," Dorian turned on the charm. "All I'm talking about is dinner. I think you're gorgeous and who cares about age?" The legions of hell were crowing. "Come on, this is the eighties. That old taboo is ancient history. I think we'd have fun. Greg in legal told me you love the outdoors. Hey, that's my main thing. I used to windboard, but now I'm getting into water skiing. You like water skiing?" He knew she did from Greg, and while he could ski he wasn't particularly fond of it. It was a ruse, and it was working.

Encouraged by her weakening refusal Dorian pulled out all the stops. "Listen, we go out, we laugh, we talk, we eat, and that's it. No harm in that."

"Cool your jets, 'cause I'm telling you this isn't going anywhere."

"Sure thing," Dorian smiled.

Kimsy Clark was pretty, with jet black hair, expensively cut, and no doubt colored, along with other work that had been done. But she was also bright, which in hindsight Dorian decided was a negative. Still, her manner was engaging, and her place in the company would be an advantage to him. She was a southern girl, born and raised on Hilton Head Island in South Carolina, and a graduate of Ole Miss. She still had a slight accent even though right after law school she took the job offer from Art Phillips and had been with him ever since. She looked all of the forty-two years behind her, but that was just fine with Dorian. In fact, everybody at Phillips looked their age, all except Dorian who stood out like a sore thumb.

Over the next few months, Dorian rarely missed an opportunity to pop in on Kimsy and flirt and fawn over her. At the annual office picnic, he met her kids: Regi four, Thyme six, and Karen seven. Nice, well-behaved kids, and Dorian acted as if he were their favorite uncle. Naturally, they liked him immediately, and Karen said exactly that to her mother who peered menacingly at her and said, "Forget about it."

Dorian plumbed Greg for more info on Kimsy swearing him to secrecy. She was crazy about Italian food and her favorite was from Riccelli's, a family-owned restaurant known for its homemade pasta and Italian "gravy." The ploy worked and Kimsy finally agreed to a date at "a good Italian restaurant in the area. Just for laughs." The tired décor put Dorian off, but this time it wasn't about him, but impressing his date. When he pulled his Porsche 911 Carrera into Riccelli's parking lot Kimsy eyed him suspiciously. "You've been talking to Greg, haven't you, you con man?"

Dorian feigned hurt. "Maybe Greg mentioned something about Italian food, but anybody with any brains knows this is the place to go for Italian," Dorian lied.

"OK, but I have my eye on you buster." She was beginning to thaw.

Kimsy had committed herself to a purely platonic relationship, and under no circumstances was she going to change her mind. "Still," she mused, "he's so cute, and friendly. My kids adore him, and he really likes me." Again, to herself, "I'm gonna make this a trial run. Any slip-ups and he's out."

They ordered drinks, Dorian his favorite Lagavulin on the rocks, Kimsy the house Chianti. As the drinks were being served Dorian opened up with jokes and small talk, his forte. "So, I get home from the gym," Dorian had continued his rigorous workout habits, "and just as I was getting dressed my crazy ass dog, Felix, whose last name is TheCat, decides he must go out. Get this. He comes into my bedroom with one of my shoes in his mouth, like he wants to dress me. I ignore him and he drops the shoe and returns with his leash. He gets up on the bed and begins to whine. What can I do? The wily critter knows I'm going out, he's to be left behind, and he's holding it over me?"

Kimsy was laughing so hard that her mascara was beginning to run.

Dorian turned the conversation to Kimsy. "So, the name Kimsy, I've never heard it before. Where'd that come from?"

"My given name is Rachel Kimberly Clark. But from day one my screwy but lovable dad insisted on calling me Kim. Trouble was, that's my mom's name, so all kinds of confusion followed. We finally confronted him, and he said to mom, 'You're my Kim,' and to me, 'You're my little Kim, my Kimsy.' I've never been known as anything other than Kimsy ever since."

Biting his tongue, Dorian listened to her life's story as if he cared, and he could immediately tell how therapeutic it was for her to open up. He rarely interrupted, and when he did it was to reassure her that she had done the right thing, that she was in the right, and that she could not be blamed for what happened. Finally, Kimsy asked, "And what about you? Who is Dorian Fist beyond the young and handsome computer wizard so good at making money for Art?"

"What's to tell? A simple Iowa boy, not from the farm." From there Dorian simply recited his concocted bio and resume, never blushing and almost believing it himself. His false openness and plausible dishonesty, along with the charm he had mastered over the years, began to win the bright but needy attorney over.

"Why no mention of lovers?" Kimsy's eyes narrowed, and her brow furrowed.

"Girls, yes, love no. At least not until recently. You can't create what isn't there."

"Until recently?"

"Yes, well, I got this job at a really good company, and I met this dark-haired beauty. But she's way beyond my league, and she had some rough romances that may have jaded her. She's just never met the right guy. You see, it's got to be magic, or it's nothing. Unless the spark turns into an inferno, well, life's too short to settle for the temperate. It's got to be fire."

"And so, who is this dark-haired beauty, and what makes you think there's enough heat left in her to light a matchstick?"

"Some women, OK, and some men, are just made cold." Dorian knew he was describing himself, but he was acting now, and he was a good actor. "But some women can never go cold. There's a natural furnace in them that can't be snuffed out. It just needs to be fanned every once in a while."

"You didn't answer me. Who is this dark-haired beauty?"

At first, Kimsy was shocked that she allowed the conversation to go this far. But she suddenly realized she wanted to hear his answer. She wanted him to say it was her. To put himself on the line that this was no mere thing but love, a lasting love that she could depend on.

"You," Dorian whispered in her ear as he stood and kissed her cheek across the table. Kimsy blushed, felt like turning away, and then gave herself over to the feelings inside her.

"This was not supposed to go this far," she cautioned. "I can't afford any more complications. I'm done with romance."

"What about love?" Dorian pursued. "Are you done with love? Who is done with love, and since when can love be turned on and off like a spigot? I'm not interested in romance, outside of the intrigue it adds to boring existence. But love is another thing. I'm caught up in this new love I have for you, and I will not renounce it."

Where Dorian found these lines he himself could not guess. Success. The goal was simply success. To overpower this force of resistance, to bend it to his will, and the course that it might take. What difference did it make? Success is measured in outcomes.

"Kimsy, you are making this all way too complicated," Dorian was laying out his personal agenda. "Tonight, we are going to make love, and tonight you will know for certain that we were meant for each other. We are going to wow the office with a sizzling courtship, followed by a spectacular wedding that will make all of them jealous."

When the Porsche pulled up to Kimsy's house the kids were already in bed. Dorian drove the babysitter home, paid, and thanked her. Then he hurried back to the house more excited at the prospect of sex than he had ever been. It had been a long while, and he had denied himself far too long while seeing to it that his future was secure.

Kimsy was waiting for him. "Scotch?" she asked. "But I don't have that, what'd you call it, Lagavulin? Will Red Label do?" Dorian's mind raced back to Pella, and it caused him to shudder.

"Sure, on the rocks, please." He was still exuding charm. Kimsy stayed with red wine. They walked out on Kimsy's small patio, among her tomato plants, flowers, and herbs. "We grew the most amazing tomato plants on Hilton Head. I've never been able to match them, but I can't kick an old habit."

"Any other habits you're not telling me about?" Dorian was always careful.

"Nothing Greg hasn't already warned you of," Kimsy teased.

"Greg again?"

"Listen, I think it's sweet you would go to all the trouble of cross-examining Greg. He doesn't know as much as you might think."

"Such as?"

"He doesn't know about the tattoo."

"What tattoo? I never saw a tattoo."

"Neither has Greg."

"You gonna show me?

"You gonna kiss me?"

"Can I kiss you on your tattoo?"

"Maybe, but for now let's focus on the lips."

Dorian took a deep breath—he knew he would dive in deep, and he wouldn't forget to kiss her tattoo just for luck. She swooned and he, the imposter Galahad, gathered her in his arms as she pointed the way to the bedroom.

Dorian made love to Kimsy as he had Stacy. He gave himself over to his primal urges. He wasn't dainty, nor was he rough. He actually preferred to be seduced and directed. He wanted to be idolized and be made love to, not make love. And he sensed the places and the ways and the timing of what would make Kimsy tremble. It was a matter of being the fulfillment of her greatest fantasy, and figuring that out made Dorian feel in control. Nor did it interfere with getting his ya-yas. The ecstasy was mutual, but the care and tenderness were on one side. Everything on Dorian's end was a fantasy being acted out. Kimsy could not have known, could never guess. This clever magician of relationships made rabbits appear from silk hats.

Kimsy's home was modest and deemed too small for five. Her divorces had taken their toll, and so it wasn't much to convince her to move with the children into Dorian's beautiful six-bedroom, four-bath home in Westwood. In addition to six bedrooms, it had a full-size swimming pool with a jacuzzi, lap pool, Har-Tru tennis court, and a built-in outdoor barbecue center tricked out like a Florida chikee hut, with water vapor outlets surrounding the patio. There was a fire pit and outdoor screen for movies.

Once again Dorian had somehow managed to create the illusion of luxurious domesticity. The kids were upgraded to private schools near Westwood, and a year after the move Dorian and Kimsy were wed. The lavish affair was held at one of the finest hotels in Des Moines, the Des Lux Hotel on Locust Street, and invited guests were restricted to Kimsy's Hilton Head family, their Phillips friends, and the small circle of carefully selected acquaintances from Kimsy's children's circles. Dorian meant to display his success and good taste. For all appearances, it seemed a marriage made in heaven.

They settled down to work and the nonstop taxiing of the kids from one thing to another. Kimsy was a gifted soprano and featured soloist and section leader at St. Peter's Presbyterian Church, downtown. She wasn't particularly religious, and never even mentioned the subject to Dorian. Rather, she was there for the music program which was outstanding. She had taken her minor in music at Ole Miss and combined her fine voice with a thorough knowledge of the sacred repertoire. Brian Gaines, the organist and music director, adored her as both person and musician. He and his partner Marco had Kimsy for dinner at least two or three times a year, and now Dorian was invited into the mix. He was reluctant seeing nothing here to advance his agenda, but Kimsy persuaded him that twice a year was something he could do for her. He went along with it. He had no idea that Brian and Marco had such a colorful and distinguished circle of friends and acquaintances, and so their dinner parties could run the gambit from interesting to downright provocative.

One party in particular became unforgettable for Dorian. During cocktails, Brian introduced him to his boss, the Reverend Norman Benchley, who was sitting next to Wesley Dadras, a professor and scholar at the University of Iowa. He was on a lecture tour promoting his new book, *The Collapse of Philosophical Foundationalism*. Dorian knew just enough of Dadras's work to anticipate some fireworks between Benchley and the professor, and he was determined to add some sparks if he could.

Dorian confessed to the pastor he knew little of the Presbyterian religion and asked for a brief rundown. Benchley complied, saying that they were of the Reformed family of faith coming out of the Reformation.

"Oh, when the church split from Rome, right?" asked Dorian.

"Correct. Perhaps Martin Luther and later with him the Lutheran Church were the first, but the Reformed followed shortly after with the teachings of John Calvin. We are of that historical line but as Presbyterians principally out of Scotland, we are a bit later and follow the rule of the Westminster Confession."

"Oh, OK, ya, the ones that replaced works with faith—that you get to heaven by faith and not by being a saint?"

"Well, that may be simplistic, but it's essentially correct." Dadras was now leaning in and listening intently. "Catholics insist we have the capacity to do good, *facere quod in se est,* so do your best and God will bless you. As such it is a gift of sorts, from God, that can allow you to perform works that might merit heaven.

However, we find that a Pelagian error and reject it entirely. It is grace alone, as a free gift, that justifies the sinner and begins the process of sanctification that leads to heaven."

Dadras could contain himself no longer. Without so much as an "excuse me," he burst in. "Ah, indeed, so there is nothing we can do to merit our salvation in your teaching?"

"Nothing."

"What about faith?"

"Say more."

"Well, isn't faith required for salvation?"

"Yes, without it there is no hope for heaven."

"And who is the source of this faith—how does it come about? Is it not a personal acceptance of Jesus?"

"That is precisely what it is."

"And is that not something that we do? In other words, as an act of will, or an acceptance of a person, namely Christ, or a proposition, namely Christianity, it is a kind of work."

"In that sense, yes."

"So then, the saved can rightly claim they have indeed secured their own salvation by an act of the will, by a personal decision. Otherwise, you are returned to Calvin's dreadful idea that God chooses the saved even before creation, without us having anything to say about it. That God, in his omnipotence and before all time, arbitrarily chooses his future friends for heaven. So, I cannot see how you can say that the believer does not secure his own salvation, in a way slightly different but not entirely different from Catholics who gain heaven with good works *and* grace."

"Well," confessed the pastor, "I suppose it is rather a matter of emphasis. Presbyterians do not deny good works, we simply put grace first."

"And what was it that led to this astonishing reversal of nearly two thousand years of Catholic teaching?" Dadras pressed him.

"Well, it was the utter impossibility of living up to Catholic standards. The sense of the Reformers was that without grace we are hopeless."

"Hopeless and evil, as in utterly depraved."

"Well, yes, filled with sin."

"But if that were the case we could do no good at all."

The preacher was silent.

Dadras went on. "Actually, we owe Luther and the other Reformers a great debt of gratitude. They merely advanced the cause of the Renaissance and led the way to the Enlightenment. What they uncovered was our deepest desire for freedom. Not just freedom from the tyranny of the Catholic order, but the freeing of our conscience, the freeing of our minds.

"Tell me, Reverend, are you a liberal thinker? I mean it appears you are accepting of the relationship of Brian and Marco, or you wouldn't be here."

"I think of myself as a social liberal and a confessional conservative. I stand by the Bible and what it teaches."

"And what does it teach about homosexuality?"

"What little it has to say is infinitely less than what it has to say about love and acceptance, not to mention not judging others," the pastor was adamant.

"Bravo. I applaud your open-mindedness. How you square the two is beyond me. Bible and love that is. But that is beside the point. My point is this, the Reformation sowed the seeds of our current hyper-pluralistic society, it led the way in demystifying the world, and so not just banishing fairies and hobgoblins but all forms of superstition. The enchanted world of ancient times gave way to the enchanted self, a new romantic vision of human potential unfettered by mythology. But the infatuation with the self was certain to lead to rampant divisiveness in run-amok pluralism. It's all so exquisitely chaotic, don't you agree? And to think such pious men brought it all on.

"Tell me, Reverend, what is it that you most despise about our culture?"

"Well, I guess I deplore its lack of faith. Faith has been replaced by materialism and deep-seated avarice. We have ceased to regard the public good, and we worship the individual. We're on our own and it's dog eat dog, survival of the fittest. I think it began with the perverse notion that the world is an accident and not God's creation. When I look at the country as a whole, I see the eclipse of humanity as a family united in its concern for the common good. I deplore the vestiges of colonialism that have led to communities of poverty, ignorance, and hopelessness. This has blinded us to our Christian obligation that creation was meant not just for the rich but all of us, rich and poor. I reel at the fact that markets act as if they are independent of morality. It seems to me tied in with the modern, crazy notion that private property is absolute, rather than something that must be subordinated to the public good. I for one am convinced that the idea of the unlicensed acquisition of material wealth works against human flourishing and impedes the way to salvation. Placing affluence above human love is blatant idolatry. It robs workers of the right to a fair wage. In that regard, I recognize with all God's people that we are our brother's keeper and put on this planet to look after each other."

"Admirable, and yet quite a list," Dadras applauded out loud rousing stares from the other guests. "You have managed to unwittingly summarize the Catholic position as circulated in the 2009 papal proclamation *Caritas in Veritate*."

"The what?" Dorian jumped in. "What do you mean, 2009?"

"Pardon, me, how silly." In the heat of the exchange, Dadras was caught off guard. "I meant to say that the proclamation is being prepared by the Vatican and due to appear shortly. No matter, you are closer to the Catholic perspective than you know, Reverend. Are you surprised that you, a liberal Protestant, might trumpet the values of the Catholic Church? And surely there is much here that I agree with. But again, to my point. Clearly, your Reformation led to all you despise about our Western culture, and yet in another curious way it led to much that you admire."

The professor went on. "As the Reformation gave rise to the Enlightenment, all your noble sentiments which tied public morality to God ceased to have any viable metaphysical foundation. Once it became clear that we cannot possibly know the divine will because we cannot possibly know the divine, we were forced to come out of adolescence and seek our truth where it can be found. That is to say, your Protestant turn toward subjectivity and toward freedom of conscience in all matters including religion led to a rigorous skepticism that pulled the foundation of Western civilization out from under it. Immanuel Kant did his best to rescue that foundation, but it was divine reason that became the only acceptable tribunal. Not God or the Bible."

Dadras held the floor. "Still, Kant's admirable attempt at a critical philosophy founded on sense experience and a transcendental logic fell apart as the scientific spirit of empiricism rejected the latter. All water under the bridge, however, now that we are left to our own devices. Still, Kant led the way in the inevitable development that we must seek what there is of philosophical truth by recognizing the limits of our understanding and paying scrupulous attention to the claims we make about reality. It was Kant's legacy to pave the way to seek philosophical precision in the use of language. To be clear about what it is that we are saying, and to expose claims that still rely on a dubious metaphysical foundation. To that end, the philosophical world remains divided by the neo-Kantians and the hapless neo-Hegelians, many of who still hold onto foundations, who still believe in the ghost in the machine."

Again, it was Dorian. "Ghost in the machine?"

Dadras chuckled, "That in the mechanisms of nature including the psychophysiology of human beings, there is an invisible substance, an infinite mind or soul, behind the workings of nature. Such are the views that still speak of God or of a transcendent reality beyond that of sense experience. You can find a frank and convincing argument for the absurdity of the God theory in Daniel Dennett's *Darwin's Dangerous Idea*, a treatment of Darwin's *The Origin of Species.*"

But Dadras wasn't finished. "The idea of a phantom spirit in the mechanism of our minds harkens to a groundless teleology that presupposes an eternal purpose or end to reasoning and life—the idea of a happy outcome. We refer to it as a *deus ex machina*. Philosophy is on the verge of abolishing such thinking, and in America for the most part we have been successful. A healthy pragmatism demands analytic approaches that seek clarity, precision, and logical rigor in our methods. Experience needs to ground itself in common-sense intuitions and how things develop and change by science, such that understanding comes by way of the standard rules of logical inference. Alas, on the Continent there remains a belligerent strain of latent *Hegelianismus* where the focus is still on the phenomena. Although they seek a thorough description of our immediate experience, they claim we have access to a kind of intuitive knowledge that goes deeper and beyond the surface of common sense and scientific experience. No one has done more to correct that aberrant way of thinking among the general public than my colleague Richard Rorty, formerly of Princeton University, now at the University of Virginia. Ah, Richard! My delightful gadfly denounced on both the right and the left, one for his dangerous relativism, the other for his conformity to the status quo. The chaos he has spawned among philosophers is positively breathtaking. His remarkable work exposed a significant failure in the Enlightenment's quest for knowledge. Philosophers wanted to organize reality such that the order of knowledge corresponded to the order of being. Richard recognized that can only be done if we can show how human action, its conflicts, relations, and activities must be as they are and cannot be otherwise. This cannot be done."

Dadras was beginning to lose Dorian but at the mention of Rorty he perked up. "Oh, ya, Richard Rorty. Listen, I've looked into Rorty. Heavy stuff, but I essentially agree with him. I think the best we can hope for is to be clear about what it is we're saying and steer clear of religious delusion. If I understood him. But a couple of things disturbed me."

"Oh?" Dadras's eyebrows curved up like horns.

"Ya, like his defense of Cardinal Bellarmine against Galileo, and Galileo's claim that the earth revolves around the sun, which Bellarmine denied. That's just plain nuts. Oh, and what about his mother? She was the daughter of a renowned pastor and theologian, Rauschen something or other, I think was his name."

"Rauschenbusch. What of it?" Dadras scoffed. "He set his daughter on the path to communism, or should I say her preferred Trotskyism. As for Galileo, Rorty was merely pointing out that until a common understanding of the planets was agreed to, there could be no firm evidence about the movement of the planets. There was nothing to convince Bellarmine that the Bible wasn't an excellent source for evidence of how the universe is organized, and so his view was equally valid as was the view of Galileo. Again, Rorty was consistent because there are many fundamentally different, genuinely alternative epistemic systems, but no facts by virtue of which one of these systems is more correct than any of the others."

"Ya, but there is his history," Dorian remained cautious. "He seemed to me at times contradictory, like when he spoke of his early experience in botany as *numinous*, and that it appeared as a vision of something of *sacred importance*. I think what he did was exchange his religious romanticism for the religion of materialism."

Dadras was incensed. "Although as a boy Rorty was caught up in the family *religion*, now rejected, he has long since jettisoned any idea of God and the transcendent as something untenable."

"Why must that be so?" This time it was Benchley weighing in. "If what you say about the limits of knowledge is true, it is certain that there are many things we do not know. And one may be that there is a God."

Dadras wasn't having it. "Rorty was simply saying that nothing can be known of such things. Which, alas, leaves a great deal to the imagination, but imagining is all it is."

"Still, that's some serious baggage to carry," Dorian pondered. "And then to end up pretty much rejecting Marxist philosophy but remain an atheist?"

"Dialectical economics when deconstructed is simply another belief system," Dadras insisted.

"That is one thing we can agree on," intoned the pastor. "But well beyond Marxism as a philosophy, what about all the evil it spawned?"

Dadras was on the defensive. "The problem of evil remains perhaps the greatest philosophical argument against the God theory of them all and not the other way around. You can't escape the dilemma before you. If there is a God, he is the source of evil," Dadras sneered. "Marx and his kind accepted the fact of evil, as we all should. But the idea of a garden before the entrance of evil into the world is a childish myth, a fiction that has plagued humankind, and as such is the real source of evil."

"But how could we possibly consider evil's source without presuming the possibility of the good?" Benchley observed. "And where else could this good exist outside of God himself? In fact, how could anything be good without God? It seems to me you set up a straw dog, and it can only lead to chaos. Without a passion for the good we doubt that anything really makes a difference. What aid might we bring, what help? Everything is mere semblance, relative, without substance, without relationship—indeed there is no subject, but only the predicate, only that you are what you say you are."

"I can live with that," Dorian chimed in.

"You go too far, Reverend," countered Dadras. "It's a shame we evolved as Feuerbach described, projecting the perfections of human nature onto an imaginary being, instead of realizing immediately what Protagoras said, that we alone are the measure of all things. In current philosophical terms, *God* is a code word for the tweaker of the cosmos, the penultimate value by which theologians deceive people. In fact, *God* for them is merely a replication of their own historical and moral designs. That urge, earlier addressed by Feuerbach, has been replaced by our experience of the deeper self. Modern psychology recognizes that our central control unit is merely a vessel of pleasures, where from birth to death and determined by our genes, we are guided by the suprachiasmatic core of the hypothalamus."

To Dorian's relief dinner was served and the guests seated such that he, Dadras, and Benchley could not continue their conversation. But Dorian felt more convinced of his practical, no-nonsense philosophy than ever. He was satisfied that when it came to the question of ethics, the outline demonstrated a huge lacuna. "Just as well," he thought. He remembered reading *Darwin's Dangerous Idea* and noting how the last section on ethics was practically nonexistent. A lot of wacky talk about game theory. "No Pharisaism in that corner," he mused. "What is it about Dadras that seems familiar?"

5

THE SANDS LAS VEGAS,
NEVADA, 2000

FIFTEEN years had passed since Dorian had come to the Phillips Company. He continued to occasionally dabble in philosophy as he sat poolside, that is when he wasn't working which was most of the time. He was still a celebrity at Phillips always pushing the envelope. Once again, his sense of timing was uncanny. Paying close attention to the oil crises, one after another, made him aware that it might be time to look beyond fossil fuel engines and consider electric cars. Still, it was a hard sell to Art, but Dorian had proven himself time and again, and so he was given the green light. He began looking into several designs and thinking about how to make electric commercially viable. At the turn of the century, there were more electric powered vehicles than their fossil fuel driven counterparts. But the range of these vehicles would make them impractical with the expansion of roads and infrastructure. Moreover, gasoline powered automobiles were becoming increasingly more affordable. It was all about range, affordability, and infrastructure. Once again, the lucky guesser at the leading edge of technology was rewarded for his pioneering efforts by the state of California. Their Air Resources Board pushed hard for fuel-efficient, low-emissions cars. Dorian secured a contract with GM for Phillips, and the result of their collaboration was the EV1. GM botched the marketing side of things, and it proved a fiasco, but Phillips Company was being well paid and simply provided the design specifics that facilitated development. The EV1 was never commercially successful, but the trade recognition of Phillips was another boon to the company. Dorian and Phillips Company would lead the way in much of the growing interest in electric, and it occupied a great deal of Dorian's time and energy. For the moment he lost sight of the fact that the company was seeing an influx of new, young professionals. The old guard was aging and several retired, but Dorian was so caught up in the chase after success he didn't notice.

Kimsy was content if mystified with Dorian. Everything he did seemed acceptable, but she couldn't dismiss a sense of emotional distance. She felt it was deeper than his idiosyncrasies, like his abnormal obsession with mirrors. He would go to lengths to appear to walk past one without looking, but the overpowering need to see himself was almost comical, contorting himself as he diverted his eyes without moving his head.

"Surely he's not sociopathic," she thought to herself, "because he's so engaging. But could it be an act?" Not without the greatest of effort. And his credulity at flattery seemed so out of keeping with his over-the-top self-confidence. Then there were his eyes, so dark, and when she looked deep into them she could see no light at all. But what remained hidden even to Kimsy was his vigilance against anything that might suggest he was aging.

Art sent Dorian to Las Vegas in the fall of 2000 to attend an automobile convention. He had a room at the famous Flamingo on the strip, but he couldn't sleep. What was it he heard just before he grabbed his flight that reminded him so much of his hasty departure from California years ago? Right, the day before yesterday he was walking past some of the old timers when he heard one of them say something like, "Oh my God, a gray hair in Dorian's beard. Impossible! He's like Peter Pan, he'll never grow old. Ha, ha, ha."

Aloud Dorian vowed, "There's no gray at all. Nor will there be." He picked up the razor and shaved. But the comment about the gray hair, the arrival of the young up-and-comings at Phillips, the growing circle of younger guests at the parties hosted by Brian and Marco, and the obnoxious, callow social climbers needling their way into the tight circle of friends, all of it was unnerving him. Silently he swore, "This is so wrong. It's all closing in on me. They think they can drag me down with them, down into complacency. To take what they believe to be inevitable. But it's not inevitable. I've proven that, and I will prove it again."

Yes, he had done it once, and he would do it again. Disappear and reappear ageless once more, in command and adored by an old guard that worshiped him. But it had to be just the right company. He was forty-eight now, but that could be overcome. Plenty of older firms out there with longtime employees. Now whispering, "But where, where can I go, where can I find peace of mind, security? A place where I truly belong. A place where I can be myself. Ah, perhaps the convention can provide the answer. Of course, the convention."

He was sent to the convention to connect with the people and companies that Phillips could do business with. All that would change. Indeed, he would network, but only to find an individual or firm that would suit his purposes. "Still, how can I do that without giving up my little secret?" Dorian pondered. "I can't be Dorian Fist from Iowa, not without giving too much away to meddlesome ears. I need to keep a low profile and learn what I can."

He left the room and took an elevator. "Strawberry Fields Forever" was plaguing the captive few on their way down. "Mind-numbing nonsense," thought Dorian. "Why must flap accompany our every movement?" Sure enough, the door opened to the third floor, completely taken over by automotive salespeople, vendors, and executives, and Dorian's senses were immediately assaulted by the heavy metal of Splatter entirely drowning out the sterilized Beatles' arrangement.

> I'd chew his ear and carve his nose
> Spit out the blood and smile

I'd kick his ass and break his jaw
Because a prick like that is better off dead
My boot would lay him flat
I could care less about this shit
I'd take him out for nothin'
Because a punk like him is a waste of time

"So much for nothing to get hung up about." Dorian was appalled. Muttering to himself, "These business bozos, look at them, boppin' and jivin', tapping their feet and shuffling the floor, to a lyric that would scandalize them if they only knew; a subculture that considers them scum. Worse than scum, the dead old establishment. But of course, they don't understand a word the band is saying. All just noise!"

No one could make out that obscure racket unless he looked it up, as Dorian had when he was exploring background music for a car commercial back when the band made a name for itself in the early eighties. Its over-the-top edginess worked well with his concept. As for the lyrics, indecipherable just like the convention. And even if they did understand, what difference would it make? "It's all so pointless," he conceded. "Just distracting amusement with no other purpose than to drown out a silence that might frighten them."

"Bars." Dorian noticed at least four within sight and booths with cars and scantily dressed female model types passing out info. "They know shit about cars. Bait for the mostly male crowd," he sneered. "Is anything ever accomplished at these carnivals?"

He grabbed a Lagavulin and made his way to the main lecture room to hear the leading authority on determining a company's worth. Reginald Foster, professor of economics at Ohio State University, was one of the few privileged elites allowed early access to IBM's supercomputer the 7030. He came up with an elaborate and highly successful program that determined a company's worth beyond assets and liabilities, and it made him a bit of a superstar in the field. He was the keynote speaker. Dorian wondered whether he would share any of his secrets with the convention. But what he heard disgusted him.

Foster was affable, self-assured, and humorous. He smiled a lot, maybe too much, leading Dorian to question his sincerity. But what he said left him completely dumbfounded. Foster opened with a question. "What is your bottom line?" He let that question sink in and during his pause, he thoughtfully paced. Then he asked, "Is it a number? Is it a figure? Is it a product?"

"This guy is a good actor," Dorian sneered.

"Is your bottom line a matter of money?" Another long pause. "No, your bottom line is your customers. And your product is customer service." In a smooth and essentially convincing way, Foster outlined his speech which had nothing to do with profit, efficiency, or marketing, none of the things Dorian expected.

"A fucking lecture on the Golden Rule, unless I'm mistaken." Dorian was incredulous. "Is he kidding? They paid this joker thousands of dollars for this horseshit?" A wave of frustration swept over him. "How in the hell can these idiots be so naive as to put up with this crap?"

Foster when on. "Beyond your customers, your bottom line is your people. They too must be of utmost importance to you. You need to treat them well, make sure they are fairly compensated, and help them secure their future. Ask them about their kids, and listen when they speak." And then he uttered the words that again grated on him, although it didn't surprise him. Foster looked at his audience, paused scratching his head in a sage gesture, looked down at his shoes for a moment, and then up and said, "What I'm really saying here is do to others as you would have done to you."

"That's it then," Dorian slammed his scotch glass to the floor startling the man in the seat next to him and scattering ice everywhere. He got up, walked out, and made a beeline for the nearest bar. He drank until he forgot about Foster and began to work out a plan. For the next two days, he would mingle quietly and carefully. Maybe sit near small groups and listen to see if he could pick up any tips.

"Tomorrow then," he whispered. Tomorrow he would put his plan into action. Content, he decided to try his luck at blackjack. Ambling up to a table with only one other player, Dorian sat down and did a double take when he realized the other player was Foster. Dorian placed his bet as did Foster, and the cards were dealt. A dozen hands later it was clear that Foster was winning big time and Dorian losing miserably.

"Ordinally I like to play alone, but I don't mind two if no more." Foster was smiling that big smile of his.

They played in silence, and Dorian noticed that Foster was intensely focused on the game. Instead of a shoe, the dealer dealt from a single deck. It seemed that at a certain point, Foster would increase his bet, and from the size of the stack of his chips he knew exactly what he was doing. But before his winnings grew extravagant he made one last generous tip and began gathering his chips. The dealer gave him a knowing smile. "The guy's a card counter or I'm a Vegas hooker," Dorian surmised. "Can I buy you a drink, Dr. Foster?" Dorian asked just as Foster got up from the table.

"I don't see why not, but looking at your stack, maybe it is I who should buy the first round," Foster flashed that formidable smile.

"No, Doc, it's on me."

"Have it your way."

They cashed in their chips then strode up to the nearest bar and ordered, Dorian his favorite peaty scotch, Foster a Manhattan. "Sweet with extra cherries," again that smile and a wink at Dorian.

"What's that about?" Dorian pondered.

"Oh, and Luxardo Cherries if you have them." Turning to Dorian, "I have a sweet tooth," Foster confessed. "So, did you enjoy the lecture? I noticed you left early."

"Is that why he agreed to this little party?" Dorian thought to himself. His cynicism was only slightly less marked than his hubris. "No, no, I have a bladder problem," he lied. "It was outstanding, just what the industry needed to hear. Listen, Dr. Foster, I know this is none of my business, but there was more than luck in play at that table this evening?"

"Call me Reginald," another smile. "Well, let us just say I have a photographic memory, and I am very good at math. My system is relatively simple. I know when the deck is hot and when it is cold, which is to say when there are more high cards, face cards, tens, and nines."

"But I thought your kind aren't welcome at casinos. In fact, I was under the impression they can spot counters a mile off and won't let them play."

"True, to a point. Don't you doubt they know very well who I am. But I get out here at most twice a year. I never win too much, and I know what too much is. I tip very well, and I drop a lot of money at casino restaurants, shows, and so on. They come away in the black, and I have all the entertainment I can handle for an old guy. Let's just say we have an arrangement."

"I knew it," Dorian laughed. "Anyway, I expect you get around the auto industry pretty well and see a great deal of what's going on. You wouldn't know of a more traditional, as in older and established firm, needing someone in marketing and design, oh say," Dorian looked down and saw Foster's drink, "in Manhattan?"

"Actually, I was out East on the island two weeks ago, and a company that I evaluated was looking for someone in that area. They've been around forever, maybe a bit tired but rock solid. Carriage, I think. Let's see, Carriage Automotive and Design. That's right."

"Hmmm," said Dorian, "Interesting. Hey, listen I've got to go. Thanks for the conversation." Dorian was already up and moving toward the elevator, briskly dropping the money for drinks and tip without pausing.

"No problem," smiled Foster, "but I didn't get your name."

"No, you didn't," answered Dorian. This time it was his turn to smile.

Dorian was back on the job on Monday. His first task was to learn all he could about Carriage. Sure enough, Foster was right but "tired" was putting it mildly. They appeared dead in the water, and in desperate need of fresh ideas. He was able to get a line on their people. Right on the money again. Judging from pictures and profiles he was looking at an average age of about fifty-five.

"No wonder they're the walking lame."

On Tuesday morning he took up the next item of business and applied for the position at Carriage based on the job description. He emailed a cover letter with his stellar fake resume, complete with a formidable cast of references. Of course, he would personally receive and reply to the inquiries under all the aliases he had created. He got a call back on Wednesday morning on his newly acquired New York number. "Dorian Fist," he crooned.

"Mr. Fist, this is Charles Gatsby of Carriage Automotive and Design. I'm the CEO. I have your resume on my desk, and I must say it is quite impressive. Might we set up an interview, oh say, this Friday, 10 a.m. in my office?"

"I'd be delighted," Dorian replied. "I'll see you on Friday. It's not far from my apartment."

The next order of business was to move almost all the money in savings and investments to his Swiss account, effective on Wednesday. "She gets the house, what more does she want?" His conscience was cleared by a vicious disdain for whatever or whomever might stand in his way. As for Art, "I made the son of a bitch rich, and he doesn't even have to thank me personally. My parting gift." Dorian went home confident that by Thursday he would no longer be Dorian Fist of Des Moines Iowa, but Dorian Fist of New York City. Job or no job, Dorian was gone, and Dorian would be reborn.

Carriage was located in the business district of lower Manhattan on the corner of Nassau and Pine. He booked himself into the classic Beekman Hotel near the Brooklyn Bridge under an alias. He liked its old-style elegance matched with modern comforts. Also, it was not far from Carriage. On Wednesday he purchased a one-way ticket for Thursday morning, first class, into JFK under the same alias and forged ID. He told his secretary he was not to be disturbed and went to his keyboard. The task of erasing his Iowa identity was much easier than before. The paper trail was essentially nonexistent. What there was of it was bought and paid for. The rest was wiped out with his hacks.

Around noon Kimsy went to see him but was told by Dorian's secretary he was not to be disturbed *by anybody*! "That's not like him," Kimsy thought. That night she asked him about it, and he told her he was in with Art, and that Art wanted his feedback on his draft new vision statement for Phillips. He was clever in using that alibi because that was precisely what Art was currently working on, and everybody in the office knew it. It was ironclad.

"So?" she pried.

"Well, I could tell you, but then I would have to kill you." Dorian let out a laugh. "No, really, he swore me to secrecy. But between us, it's a visionless vision. He's infatuated with Iacocca, who is infatuated with De Tomaso. He wants to bring them together to build a hybrid Chrysler/Maserati. It's part of his *vision* to make Phillips an international company. But it's like making a silk purse from a sow's ear." Dorian had learned of Art's plan weeks before.

"Did you tell him that?"

"No way, why should I? Listen," Dorian's deception knew no bounds. "It's time you and I found greener pastures. Hey, I'm beat. I'm gonna do a few laps in the pool, eat, and turn in early. We can talk more this weekend."

Kimsy left for work early the next morning mystified by the greener pastures comment. It was a portent dreamed up in Dorian's imagination but far too opaque for Kimsy to decipher. He packed a small suitcase and took a cab to Des Moines International Airport. He spent the time on the flight studying Manhattan. It would be a challenge to appear local, so he needed to be careful until he perfected his new identity. He arrived a little less than four hours later, took a cab to the Beekman, checked in, and made dinner reservations. He would treat himself to an evening at the iconic Oyster House in Grand Central Station. He was already beginning to feel reborn.

After dinner, he decided to take a cab to Times Square and look around. He knew nothing of the transformation that had taken place. Out West the impression was that Times Square was a cesspool, one gigantic brothel. But in the nineties Mayor Rudolph Giuliani and several New York City developers created the Times Square Alliance. They declared war on the seedy businesses in an all-out and commercially successful campaign to attract tourists.

Over the next ten years, the triple X bars and cinemas were closed, and a new vintage of theaters showing such feel-good hits as Mary Poppins made Broadway Times Square the theater capital of the world. Dorian had always thought nothing could compare to Las Vegas when it came to lights and signage, and maybe that was true of the heyday of neon. Years before he flew into Las Vegas from Chicago at night, and during the descent he was aroused from his sleep. He rubbed his eyes and did a double take. For a moment he thought the sun was rising in the West. But it was the brilliance of the Vegas neon that fooled him. Now, however, he saw an even more spectacular display of color and light, signs using the new LCD technology that turned night into day. Exhausted, he took a cab back to the Beekman and paused only long enough to enjoy a Lagavulin at the trendy bar before heading for bed.

Carriage Automotive and Design's office was bromidic. Its drab interior seemed out of character with the buzz of sleepless, electrified New York City. He would attend to that. He met Gatsby on the dot and was congratulated for his promptness, "a dying virtue," bemoaned Gatsby, and the interview began. Gatsby was about sixty, a bit flabby with a receding hairline, goatee, and mustache. His apparel was pure Brooks Brothers. "They're living in the stone age," Dorian moaned to himself. But a single click of his internal switch and charm flooded the room with artificial light and Gatsby was won over.

"I can only say that your personal presence is even more impressive than your resume. I am curious though, and I need to be honest. You are young and successful, and Carriage is old and struggling. Many of our people are looking back and not forward. Is that going to be a problem?"

For a moment Dorian lost touch with reality. Gatsby's words were alchemical. A kind of incantation of powerful magic. The experience was visceral for Dorian, and blood surged through his veins, his temples pulsed, he breathed heavily, and he rolled his head back. His eyes flickered red and yellow, and then he composed himself. Gatsby seemed not to notice.

"Mr. Gatsby . . ."

"Call me Chuck."

"Chuck, let me be honest *with you*," Dorian lied. "I grew up on Superman, the Flash, Wonder Woman, and Batman. I have a serious hero streak. I want to save the automotive world, beginning with Carriage. Frankly, although successful where I was, I didn't feel challenged. And they had zero team spirit. They were only in it for the money. Now, look, I like money as much as the next guy, but is that all there is? Not for me. I need a sense of purpose."

Gatsby was taken in. "OK then. We have a very small human resources team here that I will need to check with. They will follow up with your references. If your people get back to HR promptly we can do this in a week. But let's talk money."

In a short while and with just a little back and forth, the deal was struck, and Gatsby agreed that if it took the week that they both thought it would to arrange everything, Dorian could start the following week. "Would that be OK, Mr. Fist?"

"Please, call me Dorian," he schmoozed. "After all, we're nearly brothers in the faith now, aren't we? I'm eager to move Carriage to the front of the pack, and make her a leader in automotive marketing and design."

"We're agreed then, and I bid you good day. I look forward to seeing you in a week's time. When you come in I will have the contract ready to sign."

"Great," agreed Dorian, "But one more thing. Might I have a little tour? Just something to connect me with Carriage and its people. Would that be all right, Chuck?"

"Of course, it would be my pleasure." The tour was brief enough, just enough to confirm everything Dorian had anticipated. Carriage was an aging company. By the look of the place, most of them appeared well on their way to retirement. There were a few younger secretaries and staff but by and large it was as Dorian had surmised, an average age of about fifty-five. That would do nicely.

Dorian spent the week finding a swanky, furnished New York apartment in midtown. He hired a top real estate firm and put in a bid well above the asking in order to move the deal forward. He was in a hurry. Meanwhile, he was enjoying the Beekman spending most of his time learning how to be a convincing New Yorker.

Kimsy came home on Thursday, made dinner, and waited for Dorian. They were empty nesters now. Reg was a freshman at Iowa State where Thyme was a senior. Karin had taken an internship in Boston after graduating from Boston College. When Dorian failed to arrive Kimsy made several calls, mostly to friends and her South Carolina family. Nothing. She went to bed but couldn't sleep. The next morning, she went to work and began asking questions. When she found out that Dorian had never met with Art she began to panic. Finally, she called Missing Persons and got nowhere. She took a week off work to try and make sense of what was inconceivable, that her husband had abandoned them. Reg and Thyme drove home together, and Karin flew in the next day. The crushing tragedy and nagging uncertainty would have left them unhinged were it not for their tight bond. They clung in desperation to one another. When one fell apart, the other became consoler. And on it went.

On Friday Brian's partner, Marco Farias, stopped in to see Kimsy. The minute she saw him she broke down crying. "Marco, this is all so insane. He's gone. Just gone. Not a word, not a clue. Why?"

Marco hugged her long and hard. He took a tissue and dried her eyes. "I'm heartsick for you. I can't in my wildest imagination comprehend what you are going through."

Kimsy was still sobbing. "I can't work, I can't sleep, and I have this terrible thought that the last twelve years of my life are a lie, a complete waste. I've called everybody on the planet. I've even hired a detective. He couldn't find anything, and he told me there was no such person as Dorian Fist from Iowa. Is this some kind of nightmare? Am I going crazy? I feel like I'm in the twilight zone. I don't know whether to be scared or sad. Marco, I can't start over, it hurts too much to think about. I couldn't see this coming. I couldn't see this coming. I couldn't see . . ."

Now she was livid. "He did this you know. He took our money, our savings. How could he do this? I mean just say it's not working out. Just fess up, talk to me, I'm a big girl. I've been there before. But this is demonic. This is ruthless, and he did it to my kids too. The bastard." Anger out it was time for more sobbing. What followed was self-recrimination.

"No, I'm not to blame. This won't fall on me. I didn't, I wasn't, I never . . ."

"I'm going to make you some chicken soup," Marco suddenly got up and went to the kitchen.

"Chicken soup?" Kimsy looked at him incredulously through bloodshot eyes and running mascara.

"It helps fix most everything," Marco smiled. "My mom said it has medicinal properties. I don't know about that, but I find that when nothing can be said and nothing can be done, chicken soup comes to the rescue." For the first time in a week Kimsy laughed.

The next few years of Kimsy's life were challenging. She had a great shrink, and her inner strength and courage were remarkable. Tom Conrey was a blind therapist working out of a small office in Des Moines. More than a great bedside manner, he was brilliant and brought to bear all the skills of his profession. His gradual but relentless hereditary vision loss was replaced by an uncanny inner vision into the heart and soul of his patients. Counseling had become more art than science for him. No school, no one approach, no instant cures or success. It was the listening, the measured advice, and the sense of genuine concern. It was the help with decision-making, the unpacking and repacking of the baggage in a more manageable order. It was the slow and steady strengthening and reinforcement of the desire to live and to live without pain.

The kids spent months in therapy as well, but they had lives to live and a strong will to move on. The support of their mom knew no bounds, and she drew strength from them. They spoke every day, and soon the conversation was no longer about Dorian but about their lives, their loves, and what mattered to them. And now what mattered to them most mattered most to Kimsy. She spent more time with her Hilton Head family. She thought about giving up her music, but Brian and Marco would have none of it. Instead, Brian began featuring her even more often at Sunday worship. She threw her heart and soul into her craft. Before, music was merely a pleasurable part of her life but really just a hobby. Now music became her salvation. Besides her children, it was the curative that brought her back from the brink of emotional death.

Two years after Dorian's disappearance Kimsy performed Bach's aria, "Sheep May Safely Graze."

> Sheep may safely graze and pasture
> In a watchful Shepherd's sight.
> Those who rule with wisdom guiding
> Bring to hearts a peace abiding
> Bless a land with joy made bright.

Marco came to her afterward and said her voice had reached a new level of intensity and authenticity. He said, "Kimsy, you know that Bach is without mercy; that he has only the slightest consideration for performers because he deemed every note essential. He insisted that only with flawless execution would the beauty of the notes reveal themselves. Your performance today was flawless. So beautiful, I am truly at a loss for words. Kimsy, you are just fabulous, and I am so, so impressed. I am so, so proud!"

Kimsy hugged him and kissed him and cried. Marco whispered,

> The dross consumed your heart was pierced
> Gold refined in tempering furnace fierce

"What is that?"

"Nothing," said Marco. "I will see you at dinner this Friday. And don't be late," he teased.

What suffered most for all of them was their ability to trust. The ability to lean on others and confide in them was severally shaken and outside of the immediate family, they each added a layer of protective suspicion of even the ones they loved. Kimsy swore off men forever. Or, as she told her now dearest friend Marco, "Marco, I will never again fall in love. Well, at least until tomorrow," sweetly channeling the spirit of the Hal David lyrics. She laughed, and Marco stared at her for a moment. Her humor was part of her resilience. He blinked and looked again and saw his friend in a new light, and so he laughed with her. His thoughts silently drifted to Dorian. "Does he have any idea at all what he's lost, what he's given up? This treasure, this priceless treasure?"

Art Phillips took it hardest at the company. At first, he thought Dorian had been kidnapped, and that he would soon be receiving a ransom note. He still believed in Dorian and would stretch his neck out to the extreme to exonerate him. But there was the lie about the visit to Dorian's office. Perhaps Dorian's single tactical error. When he persisted, Kimsy told him what she had told no one else, not even the kids. That Dorian had emptied out their savings. The evidence proved unassailable. Art succumbed to seething anger, anger at being betrayed. He lost focus and decided to retire which led to a nervous breakdown. Once again therapy and time healed him enough to find some semblance of peace in his retirement. But the scars were deep and lasting. The question of *why* was like a dagger digging into his flesh leaving a wound that would not heal.

6

MANHATTAN, NEW YORK, 2000

WITH Dorian providing a quick reply to HR's emails, Gatsby got the green light and called Dorian in the next week as promised. Contract signed Dorian asked if he could start the next day. He was eager to discover the source of Carriage's inertia. That proved easy, they had run out of ideas and ambition. With an empty field ripe for tilling, he dug in. His early experience with airbags convinced him that the future of the industry was safety, and that led him to begin work on a tire pressure monitoring system. Sure enough, although Porsche installed a system on the 959 supercar in the late eighties, it took the outrage brought about by the Firestone-equipped Ford Explorer rollovers to force new laws making wide use of the system necessary. Dorian was right there moving the industry from an Indirect Tire Pressure Management System as on the Porsche 959, to a Direct Pressure Management System, with monitoring sensors inside each tire. By 2000 laws would ensure that all future cars were equipped with the technology. Carriage's son had risen.

At about the same time and in a similar fashion, Dorian was exploring OBD I, the first onboard diagnostic system. The design was right up Dorian's alley with his superior computer and engineering expertise. OBD allowed mechanics to discover much more easily what was wrong with a vehicle. Early on car lovers hated OBD because they felt its only purpose was to test emissions. Dorian's design of OBD II changed everything, leading to dramatic improvements in automobile performance, as well as their running cleaner. In addition, Carriage was able to lead the way in marketing scanning tools for diagnostics and also aftermarket devices including performance tuners and fuel economy meters.

The company was once again a contender. But the technology that put them over the top was Dorian's work on the dual-clutch transmission. His first concept to design took a lesson from the auto racing world, which as early as the eighties was successfully experimenting with dual-clutch transmissions. Dorian designed a way to move that from the track to the street, but it was a hard sell. He finally convinced Gatsby to look abroad, and they approached Volkswagen with the concept and a rudimentary design. His flawless German and brilliant computer models suggested that the instability of the dual clutch could be overcome with time and technology. They liked the idea and promised Carriage they would handle the marketing when the design was made available to the public.

Dorian was once again a legend among his peers. His feigned humility as he strode the halls of Carriage made him feel almost moral, and the compliments drew him into thoughts of immortality. Still, he typically kept his patent porker face at the comments. "You did it again, Dorian." "You kid, are a certifiable genius." "Dorian, we were on life support. Your smarts brought us back from the brink. You not only saved the company but our pensions. Grats!" His impassive expression betrayed no vanity, while inside his conceit knew no limits. "But, hey, Dorian, one thing nobody can understand is how someone so young can have so much experience. To know where the trends are heading. Remarkable. How do you do it?"

Dorian reeled, became flush, and then composed himself. The fawning always spawned a visceral reaction in him, and it was a powerful potion. Intoxicating. No, more than that, it was bewitching like an incantation and in his twisted amoral reasoning, it was confirmation that he had made the right move relocating to New York.

Once again his work and what it brought him was at the center of his life. And while success came easy to him, he punched the meter and clocked the time that was required to bring the company back from the dead. No magic involved in that, just hard work. He thought of that often. It was justification for all that he did. "These people, their jobs, their success, that's my doing. That's on my back. Were it not for me, they might be in chapter 13 by now. Instead, they're thriving. If I hadn't relocated, where would they be?"

But that meant hours at the plow and little time left outside of his workouts. However, Dorian had no intention of being alone for the rest of his life. Still, marriage was out of the question. "Too complicated," he concluded. "And what's the point? It used to be I needed respectability. Companies wanted respectable executives. Not today. Today, hell, people could care less." But coming home from work to an empty apartment every evening was getting old. What he needed was a girlfriend. "No, what I need is three or four girlfriends," he snickered, "all on a string, just to keep things interesting."

The female prospects at Carriage would never fit into Dorian's future designs, so he didn't even bother. His resume and the office gossip made him out as single and on the prowl. Word leaked with his blessing, and he began to get invitations to social gatherings from his colleagues. Occasionally these would include some matchmaking by well-meaning associates, and that worked into his agenda. He could evaluate the prospect to his satisfaction, make sure the quarry was pretty, visibly older than he, and what he considered his "type." It also meant that his exposure to the social world was minimal, and that was what he wanted. "Keep the publicity to a minimum, please!" he begged them.

But Dorian was wary of dating several women all from the same circle. It could only get complicated and messy. Bars are good, but he preferred to have his local and not jump from place to place. Plus, he'd run the same risk of these women knowing each other.

"Hmm, hold on here," he thought to himself. "BodyWorks." It was the name of his New York gym, a high-end fitness center with all the bells and whistles, located one floor below the famous Top of the Sixes restaurant at 666, Fifth Avenue, overlooking Central Park. He silently began to plot his course. "I've been going to the gym all my life and never doing anything other than fantasizing about the chicks there. That's one place. And then there's shopping. Women are always shopping. Also, this is New York, and what better place to meet a higher class of females than at museums, concerts, and galleries? I need to broaden my cultural horizon anyway. OK, it's a plan." Dorian would literally shop around.

His first date after coming to New York was with Connie Matthews, an extrovert and a poser, a girl lined up by the Carriage crowd. Glen Baskins in HR threw a cocktail party at the insistence of Celeste Holmes, a married fifty-two-year-old who would repeatedly hit on Dorian without success. "My God, Celeste, I play golf with your husband. Are you out of your mind?"

Celeste felt called to bring some happiness into Dorian's "miserable existence," and she had a flair for the dramatic. Striking out with Dorian, she decided she had just the person in mind, Connie, a high school friend from way back. Celeste went off to college, Connie pursued the spotlight, and after years of getting nowhere in theater and films gave up on auditions. But Celeste and Connie kept in touch.

Of course, Connie knew why she was there, and Dorian knew it too. He had already passed by two candidates, the first being younger and so frightening to him, and the second simply talked too much. Connie was the same age as Celeste, curvy, maybe just a little fleshy, and very attractive. She knew how to dress, and she was immaculately coiffured. They were introduced, and Dorian wasted no time ushering her to the bar where Connie asked Glen for a scotch on the rocks. Dorian lit up and leaned over to Glen. "I'm feeling lucky tonight. You don't happen to have my favorite Scotch, Lagavulin, do you?"

Glen laughed at the inside joke. "Sorry, never heard of it. I'm a vodka man—but I do have Glenlivet."

"That will do perfectly, on the rocks old man," he teased, yet believing it with every ounce of fiber in him.

Connie told Dorian she worked at Macy's in their perfume department. That fit. She was doll-like with her impeccable make-up job. Skin tone, lip color, eye shade, and mascara, all perfect, just as he had witnessed on numerous occasions passing through the aisles of upscale department stores with their bevy of beauties pumping perfume and painting faces. When shopping he would go out of his way to include a saunter through jewelry and cosmetics, and he marveled at the number of mirrors that surrounded him.

To get the ball rolling Dorian lied that he hadn't missed a single Macy's Thanksgiving Day Parade in a decade. Connie laughed and replied that she made it a point to be out of town that day. She said retail had turned her into a Grinch, and she had come to hate the holidays. "But I'm fine with Groundhog's Day," she joked. They dated off and on, with Dorian calling the shots. He made it clear to Connie that she was on notice, any misstep on her part would end their relationship. But Connie was no fool; in fact, she was as self-centered and manipulative as Dorian. "If this asshole thinks he's got me under his thumb," she snarled to herself, "he's got another thing coming. Shit, he's rich, young, good-looking, got a great body, and likes to spend his money. His apartment is practically a mansion, and he can be fun to be with. As long as I'm having a great time on his dime, fuck him. And I will." But when it came to sex and the overall quality of their relationship, it was a zero-sum game.

Still, Dorian was one to stick to his game plan, and even as he began dating Connie he was looking around. The next stop was the gym. He had already checked the scene out and had a couple of candidates. The first was a tall, ginger-haired girl in her early fifties. Carrie Prentice had a no-nonsense attitude about her workouts and socialized little if at all. She was married but that meant nothing to Dorian unless it led to unwanted drama. After a month, he realized she liked his flirtatiousness, but it became clear she was simply enjoying the attention and had no desire to carry it any further. He began to avoid her.

His second choice was a woman heavily into yoga who always followed up her weekly class with a light workout with weights. When there was no class she worked out on the stationary bike or took a spin class. In every way, she embodied Dorian's stereotype of the "yoga mentality," or seemed to. She was slender, fifty-one years old, "underfed," Dorian quipped, and properly uniformed, exclusively wearing tight-fitting NamuGoddess outfits with a modest amount of skin showing. Her hair was done up yoga style, tied up in a neat ponytail to keep it out of the way and in reasonable shape after all the posing.

He found out later she was in sales, and it was reflected in her impeccable dress. Her footwear upon arrival was like that of professional athletes, especially tennis stars, brand-new, colorful sneakers, Adidas, Nike, and the like, changed out well before their expiration date. She made a ritual of removing her shoes before class and so entered the studio barefoot. She would throw her head back, breathe deeply, and bend down to remove her shoes symbolically leaving the outside world behind and entering the inner, spiritual world of Nirvana. She made a point of placing them on the shoe rack toes facing out, as if to say, I will return to continue my journey. She never left the class early, always put her cell phone in her gym bag outside the studio, and reverently bowed hands clasped, "Namaste," invoking the traditional greeting of the yogi and her classmates.

Dorian noticed that unlike several of the students, she never looked at the other practitioners' poses who seemed bent on comparing themselves, or sizing up the competition, or simply acting insecure. She was clearly given over to the experience. But she might as well be; she was pretty, good at the art, and her body was exceptionally fit. She didn't need to feel inadequate or in need of help. She seemed genuinely lost in the moment.

Diana Hastings was always early for class and everything else, seeing to it that she never crowded another member of the session nor wasted a client's time in her work. At the head of the class was the yogi, a young male in his thirties with long, curly brown hair but cleanly shaven, who practiced without a shirt. Before each session he sat in lotus position, demonstrating his controlled breathing and incidentally showing off his six-pack. Dorian thought that for someone dispassionate about the careworn world, someone who had jettisoned his ego, he was awfully proud of his stomach muscles. He was given to tossing out New Age platitudes which seemed to mesmerize his students.

Diana carried her mat as if it were her magic carpet, an enchanted rug, which she would enthusiastically throw open and then slowly and gently massage, leisurely taking her time smoothing the organic cotton (everything she owned was organic), *yog chatai* into position. Then she would approach it and not so much sit on it as mount it. Her focus was intense, and she never once noticed Dorian watching her. She invariably produced a pink cotton towel to dry off after class, daintily dabbing at her brow and cheeks which hadn't a trace of sweat, and she always thanked the yogi. However, she remained personally aloof and never engaged her fellow practitioners other than the polite, "Namaste."

Dorian's new challenge was a top salesperson for Russell Athletic Wear. The branch office was in the Empire State Building, at Thirty-Fourth and Fifth, on the ninety-fifth floor. The view outside her window was breathtaking. Dorian approached her as she was working her triceps with the thirty-pound curl bar. "Not bad for a woman," he silently patronized. He asked if he could "work in," meaning share the curl bar, and she obliged him with a smile and a wink.

"What was that wink all about?" he wondered to himself. Dorian was always caught off guard by mysterious body language. "Is that a come-on?" he privately pondered. He no longer feared women, but he remained cautious and obsessed over subliminal messages so as to protect his fragile ego. He would take it slow.

"I've only recently seen you at BodyWorks, but it's obvious you're into fitness. So, are you new to New York?" she asked him.

He told her that although he was born and bred in Manhattan, he switched to BodyWorks because the other place had gotten too crowded. He had already visited half a dozen gyms in order to find what he was looking for, so their names were fresh in his mind. She never asked.

"No wonder I hadn't seen you until recently. Have you given any thought to yoga?"

Dorian had no intention of taking up yoga, but he said he was very interested. "In fact, I watched a couple of your classes. I gotta say, you look the proverbial lady Aladdin the way you seem to soar with your mat."

Dorian was taken back but delighted when Diana sang to him in response, "And me, I'm flyin' on my *chatai*, taking tips and gettin' toned." Her cover of the iconic Harry Chapin song "Taxi," was spot on. She pitched her class, "So why not get your own magic carpet and take a ride? You'll love the way we fly." Diana borrowed the popular slogan from Delta Airlines.

The teller of fabulous tales lied that he needed to wait until his injured meniscus completely healed. "I'm seeing a physical therapist."

Diana, the devotee and believer, said the yoga would "absolutely" help his injured knee. Dorian nodded and cautiously agreed, "Ya, that might work, just as long as I don't piss off my PT. I'm in no mood to start over with a new gal. Listen," Dorian changed the subject, "I'm done here but I hope to train with you again. Oh, and thanks for letting me work in with you."

"No problem," smiled Diana, "Hope to see you around."

Dorian made it a point to flirt with Diana every time he made it to the gym and that was most days. He made sure to adjust his schedule to coincide with hers, and they began doing a regular light workout together either after yoga or after her spin class. While she was on her mat, Dorian did his aerobics and heavy lifting. After three weeks he was ready to ask her out. She knew it was coming and was pleased to accept.

"One thing, though," Diana was curious. "Something I've been meaning to ask you. So, like, it's obvious you're interested in me, but aren't you a bit young? I mean, let's face it, I've got several years on you. I feel like I'm robbing the cradle."

Again, Dorian was elated. Words he longed to hear and at just the right moment. It was all he could do to not blush. "That old taboo has gone out with fanny packs," Dorian said dismissively. "Look, we have the same hobbies. we love staying healthy and keeping fit. What's to stop us from seeing where this might go?"

She chuckled at the mention of fanny packs, the nerdy mini packs tied around the waste that she used to swear by. "Have you given any thought to my suggestion of yoga?" she surprised him.

"Well, yes actually, I've been giving it a lot of thought," he lied, "but I'm not sure I can fit another thing into my daily routine. But why all the passion about yoga?"

"Well, if we're going to date you might as well know I'm a very spiritual person."

"Spiritual, like you go to church?"

"No, not like that, spiritual as into being connected to the universe and its energy."

"So, I guess I should ask you your sign?"

"Pleeease, spare me. My God, the oldest line ever! Pisces," she grinned. "But this age thing is an issue. Are you sure you know what you're doing?"

"I told you that kind of thinking disappeared with the Age of Aquarius."

Diana winced, scrunched her eyes, and stared. "Is he making fun of me?" she wondered. "No, it was said in all innocence," she decided.

Dorian just thought he was being clever and didn't notice her recoil. He was well rehearsed at dispelling old prohibitions. "Like I said, we're into the same things. We love working out, keeping fit, sweating to the oldies, and I have my spiritual side too. Why not give it a go?"

"Oh, and what's your spiritual side?"

"Well, let me qualify that. I'm a born-again philosopher." He chuckled and thought his mixed metaphor clever. "I mean, I read philosophy every chance I get. You see, I like to think about the big picture. You know, what's it all about and the like."

"That's not what I consider spirituality." Diana wasn't convinced. "Spirituality is being in touch with the life force that surrounds us. It's the balance of Yin and Yang. For me, it's the cultivation of my spiritual center which lifts me above mere materiality; it carries me beyond obsession with physical pleasure; it puts me on the path of escape from rebirth."

She went on, "Dorian, our souls are all part of the great chain of being powered by universal love and the goodness of all humankind. Knowing that I treasure my body as the vessel of my soul, and so I worship it and I cherish it, and I recognize a kinship with all who with me worship the synergy of body and spirit."

Dorian feigned confusion, "But I thought you were in sales at Russell?"

"What does that have to do with it?"

"I don't know, I just assumed salespeople were kinda grounded."

"I am grounded."

"I mean down to earth, like in getting well paid, pushing the product, staying on top of your game. You know, being successful."

"The two are not mutually exclusive."

Dorian was skeptical. "So, look, you go out with me and maybe you can explain how as a top salesperson for Russell you haven't sold your soul to the devil."

"Deal."

"Great! I'll come by this Friday night, around eight, with a cab and pick you up. How about the Café des Artistes?" Dorian was referring to the legendary French restaurant at One West Sixty-Seventh Street, named for the famous artists that dined there.

"Oh, wow, you're going straight for the jugular then?"

"Well, ya, OK, it's romantic, but the food is wonderful too. Not just ambiance we're talkin' here. Listen, you said you were into nature. Well, the dining room is filled with flowers." Once again Dorian thought he was oh-so-clever. "And aren't the spiritual supposed to feel a kinship with nature, like in the *au natural*? Well, we'll be surrounded by nearly two dozen nude murals. If that isn't spiritual I don't know what is."

"Don't you be getting any ideas. That's not the kind of spirituality I'm talking about, and you know it."

"Fine, I'm just excited about seeing the famous Christy murals again, and given everything you've told me, you might feel right at home among the wood nymphs." Dorian chuckled at himself but he was pressing his luck, and about to press himself out of a date.

"You think you know something about spirituality but you're way off course. All right, let's do it." Diana felt she had nothing to lose. For all the work she put into this conversation she decided she would let him pick up the check.

"OK then, we'll talk at dinner, and you can explain it all to me. See you then." He stole a quick kiss. Diana flinched, drew back, squinched her eyes like before, and said, "Next time ask."

"Promise," Doran lied.

The cab picked Dorian up at his apartment and they drove to Diana's gorgeous apartment building on Fifth Avenue. He called ahead and so she was waiting for him in the foyer. When the cab pulled up the door attendant escorted her to the cab. As they drove to the restaurant Diana was talking a blue streak, but Dorian was deep in thought. He had been reading of a company that may have the means to develop a car battery capable of a charge that would go six hundred miles. But when the radio in the cab began to play Paul Anka's "Diana" his ears perked up. He knew every word of the song, and when the singer spoke of his being so young and Diana being so old, a lightning shock went through him. He quickly looked at Diana and realized she wasn't paying any attention. A sense of relief washed over him. But why? It was his secret, one he kept locked up safely in the attic of his mind. The cab pulled up to the restaurant and for some strange reason, Dorian felt safe. Seconds later they were met by the maître d', who seated them in a secluded little alcove thanks to a generous tip from Dorian. The dining room was truly spectacular, and as he said adorned with fresh flowers. Diana ordered a cabernet sauvignon. "I don't care about the vintage, please just deep and full-bodied."

"*Oui, madame,* I have just the thing." Dorian ordered a Lagavulin on the rocks.

They perused the menu, and both decided on the prix fixe. Escargot to start, followed by turbot sauteed in lemon, tarragon, and butter with *haricots verts*. Diana wanted to switch to white wine and summoned the sommelier. They inquired after the perfect complement to the fish, and she recommended the *Matrot Meursault Premier Cru Blagny*. Her practiced French accent was precious for its fractured English. "This is for the *poisson délicat*. On the nose you can get there a distinct mix of *goût de pierre à fusil, no*? Flint but not chalky. And how you say, the crisp and light fruitiness, with just a little salt, you know, the *finir*. Perfect with turbot."

After *le plat principal* they had a simple salad with a vinaigrette. For dessert, they shared a cheese plate with fresh sliced apples and a fine old port. They talked nonstop throughout the meal.

Dorian would have preferred to stick with chit-chat about the sweltering summer, the inside scoop on the yogi, or how long the pool at the gym would be closed for maintenance, and of course sex, but Diana took him up on his challenge. After putting up with his small talk all through dinner, she pressed him on his earlier question. "OK," Dorian relented, "I give up, unravel for me the compatibility of spirituality and being a world-class salesperson?"

"How can you see a conflict here?" Diana objected.

"How can you not see one?" Dorian shot back. "Sales is all about materialism not spiritualism. Let's say you land a huge offer to buy a ton of your most garish Russell discards to a company in Georgia. You know perfectly well that the line is never going to fly in that part of the country. Do you proceed with the sale?"

"It's not for me to tell the customer what he needs or wants."

"Of course it is, you are a peddler, a merchant, a mercenary, your job is to convince them they *need* your product, whether they do or don't, and that's what you do or you wouldn't live at 956 Fifth Avenue, a godamn palazzo. You didn't get to where you are by sending people to Gimbles." Dorian was referring to the Christmas movie *Miracle On 34th Street*, where Mr. Macy sends customers to Gimbles when he hasn't got what they want. "That feel-good movie is a hoax. All 'do to others' shit. No, the point of life is to be the self-possessed salesman of the self, to recognize that when someone seeks to influence you he seeks to diminish you, steal your will to be yourself."

"The material and the spiritual can be balanced. Both have their place," she argued.

"No they can't," Dorian shot back, "and no they don't. You either think there is a God or you don't. You serve mammon or God. As for me and my house, we serve mammon." Dorian was twisting Joshua 24:15 into his own procrustean scheme.

"I believe in God."

"No, you don't! You believe in the Force. You're nothing but a modern-day gnostic. Your *god* is carefully circumscribed in brackets because it is merely a code word. Whether it's the old think of a supreme being, an unmoved mover, the ground of all feeling and dependence, or this New Age crap of an inner light, it all amounts to the same thing. The old think makes God a factor, an outcome, just another object among objects. But your god is even worse. It's an opiate, no it's your crack, 'cause it's twice as dangerous as opium."

Dorian was suddenly angry. "Listen, Diana, your irrational mysticism is a Peter Pan flight to the Never-Never-Be, it's make-believe, a leap to the imaginary, which in this case is the occult. And this self-styled god of inner light and mystical experience you toy with, well it's dangerous, uncontrollable, and it's led to more war, more harm, more destruction than you can possibly imagine. It's the delusion shared by so many of your type that the enlightened few are the messengers of heaven. In truth, your thinking amounts to nothing but therapeutic radiations, the refuge you and your kind seek for your own inability to act. 'Look within sister, look deep inside brother.' Bullshit. It's hucksterism because if you truly look within you will see nothing because there is nothing there, other than the emptiness you fill either with superstition or with pleasure. Get yourself a mirror and look again. There is nothing but the image. And these paintings you see all around you, they are just form and color; they say nothing other than look at me. So, get with it and choose pleasure."

"Listen, I've had just about enough of your bashing my faith."

"And I've had just about enough of people like you who abandon reason to take to your underground pseudo-religious bunkers. Dreaming up your alchemic false magic to lull you into stupefaction, all so you can ignore the hopelessness you feel. You want hope, you want certainty, sell the fuckin' Georgians the sweatshirts and move on. You'll feel better. And if you start obsessing over the power of evil, it's nothing other than the baggage being handed you by those who would weigh you down and drain you of your will to be who you are." Dorian's eyes appeared flaked with yellow and flashed "caution." It startled and frightened Diana.

"Since this relationship is going nowhere, I suggest you pay the bill, and we leave."

"Fine."

Not a word was said in the cab. After Diana was dropped off the driver glanced in the review mirror, caught Dorian's eye, and said, "Struck out, eh?"

"Fuck off," was Dorian's reply.

The cab driver merely chuckled.

The next day Dorian canceled his gym membership, never looking back. Diana was fuming but would have welcomed a cooling-off period with a chance for reconciliation at least in terms of friendship if nothing else. Not Dorian. He burned his bridges as quickly as he burned the pathways to his essence.

Connie called him on Thursday the next week and asked to spend the weekend. She wanted to come over on Friday, so he needed to have Ryerson Erden, the building superintendent, let her in. He called Ryerson from work and made the arrangements. When he got home Friday late afternoon Connie wasn't there. He called Ryerson, who said he had let her in but that she said she needed to do some shopping, and that Dorian told her to take the Porsche.

"What the fuck?" he screamed.

"Sorry, boss, but I took her at her word."

Connie returned at about 6:30 p.m. and Dorian was waiting for her boiling mad. "Where the hell did you get the nerve to steal my car?" he screamed.

"I needed to shop and, oh, I got groceries."

"You got shit. Get the hell out of here. I told ya, you mess with me, and you're gone. Now go."

She grabbed her things. "You know, Dorian you really are an asshole. So, fuck off and the Porsche with you."

"Ya, well don't let the door hit you in the ass," he shot back. Connie was gone. "Good riddance."

Dorian decided to swear off women and bury himself in his work. That only lasted so many years before he became seriously lonely again. "OK," he thought, "one more try, one last venue." He read that the Metropolitan Museum of Art on Fifth Avenue was holding a special exhibit called *Scenes of Eternity*. "I will resume my hunt there."

On Saturday morning Dorian caught a cab to the museum, gave his contribution, and began viewing the exhibits mostly on loan from galleries and museums all around the world. As he slowly made his way from painting to painting, taking his time, trying desperately to care, to catch something of the point of art, to feel something other than boredom, he silently confessed to himself, "I should somehow be moved by all this, but frankly I'd rather see a movie." He suddenly had a terrible sense of dread, remembering a favorite motion picture of his, the classic Japanese film *Rikyu*, about the famed Japanese tea master of the same name. The story is of the boorish shogun Toyotomi Hideyoshi, who desperately wishes to perform the tea ceremony, but whose base aesthetic sense cannot rise to anything higher than a bumbling, mediocre performance of what is quintessential to art.

Dorian looked long and hard at *L'Angélus*, an oil painting by the French painter Jean-François Millet, on loan from the Musée d'Orsay, Paris. Before him was a masterpiece showing the bowed figures of a man and woman, peasants praying at the end of the day over what appeared to be a basket of potatoes, farmers bathed in the supple, gentle light of the setting sun; an extraordinary use of light as day becomes night and the orange of the sun fades to gray. It exuded the genius that allowed a still painting to create the illusion of movement. Behind them is a church, its bell tower signaling the end of the workday. Still, it simply escaped his notice how much like a funeral scene it was. "Why is this in an exhibit supposed to be about eternity?" he wondered.

Moving on he suddenly spotted a striking woman in her early fifties staring intently at what he later learned was a polyptych, a painting, in this case, an altarpiece, with panels joined by hinges or folds. He noticed a wry grin on her face. The oil on wood was by Hieronymus Bosch, the fantastical, disturbing Dutch painter who lived around 1500, and whose sensitivity to the depths of human misery and fear was uncanny. On loan from the Gallerie dell'Accademia in Venice, it was a dark and dire piece with four panels, depicting the *Fall of the Damned, Hell, Earthly Paradise*, and the *Ascent to Heaven*. The exhibit label said the original order was unknown. It was titled *Visions of the Hereafter*, but could also be called *Cardinal Grimami's Altarpiece*.

The stranger was equally dark, suggesting she might be from India. Her features were Aryan, but her complexion was like coffee with just a small dash of cream. Her hair was jet black and braided in the Indian style. Her already dark eyes were made even darker by thick eyeliner and mascara, and the bright red she wore on her lips suggested a warning that they were impervious. She was beautiful with large breasts mostly bared and suggestively displayed by a strappy detail top. It too was black and looked as much like a bathing suit top as anything else, except that thin straps crossed the chest left to right, top to bottom, and then again smaller straps crossed below. And unlike a bathing suit top, it continued down her slender waist to slightly below the midriff and covered the top of her tight-fitting, short black skirt. Shapely legs narrowed to stiletto-sharp high heels. All black.

She seemed particularly interested in the last panel, the *Ascent to Heaven*, and according to the label it was sometimes called the *Ascent into the Empyrean*. Although it was a painting depicting the gate of heaven, it was cheerless. In the foreground winged angels were escorting the embodied but visibly sexless souls upward. Nobody appeared particularly pleased, even while the saved were staring directly into heaven depicted by a circle of light, like a tunnel. Dorian decided to make his move. He looked over her right shoulder, and being several inches taller he could easily view the last panel. She ignored him, and so he ventured his opening line. "It's pretty strange, isn't it? I wonder who this Bosch guy was?"

"Strange isn't the word for it," she answered without turning away from the panel. Her voice was melodic, perfect for temptation. "It's grotesque, but that's to be expected of Bosch. He was given to delusional art and lived at a time when life was brutal, death pervasive, misery rampant. The Catholic Church, all-powerful and beyond suspicion, ensured that things never improved. Believe me when I tell you, Bosch was commissioned and well paid for his contribution to the humorless divine comedy."

Still not looking back she teased, "But earlier I noticed you seemed more interested in the women in the museum than in the paintings."

"Am I that obvious?"

Ignoring the question, she moved on. "Let me show you a more realistic depiction." She turned to him and smiled. Still, it was a smile filled with cunning.

She walked him to the next room and to a painting by Marc Chagall called *Jacob's Dream*. Painted about 1963, it was on loan from the National Museum Marc Chagall in Nice.

"Do you know this scene?" she asked. "What it depicts, that is?"

Dorian stared intently. "Haven't a clue. Looks like chaos to me. Maybe some fairies?"

"Look more closely. The man below is dreaming, and see the ladder to his right? What do you remember about a ladder and a dreaming man?"

"Of course, Jacob's ladder." Dorian recalled the story from his Sunday school days.

"And what do you remember about that passage from Genesis?"

Dorian thought for a moment. "That Jacob dreamed about a ladder with angels going up and down. That's about it."

"Do you see what Chagall has done with that dream? Chagall is a product of his time, of a world taken leave of Bosch's angels and demons. It's a world unhinged from contact with heaven, where aspirations to transcendence are left in the hands of unreasoning cults."

Dorian was all ears. "Exactly! A world where the deluded promiscuously or often mindlessly peddle their escapist schemes of transcendence." He decided he liked Chagall.

"So, do you see how Jacob's angels in Chagall's vision are actually human figures, and instead of ascending and descending, they are pushing one another up and down the ladder? If there is to be any transcendence in Chagall's view, it comes by way of people, people who push each other up for something higher."

"I guess I'm one hundred percent with him on that, other than to say if you don't push yourself up nobody's gonna do it for you." Dorian was satisfied.

"So, what is your view of art? Sorry, your name is?"

"Dorian. Dorian Fist."

"Well, Mr. Fist, what is your theory of art, especially modern art?"

"Call me Dorian. And what is your name?"

"Kelly, Kelly Azar. So, what do you make of art?"

"Simple. As for paintings, they are simply form and color nothing more. The canvas represents nothing universal. Beauty is in the eye of the beholder. That is to say, beauty is completely subjective, and what really counts is the beautiful life. The living of art, so to speak. As for the artist, his is no different from my work. We must strive for perfection in whatever way seems best. I guess I want my life to be my art, which is why so many artists fail. They put so much into their art that they have nothing left to make life their art."

"So, you don't believe that art captures something sublime in nature and represents it in a unique way—that is to say, captures that which is transcendent in nature?"

"Not at all."

"The Greeks did just that and more. When you looked at a statue of Aphrodite as an ancient Greek, it was the goddess you saw and not simply her statue. You see, the Greeks lived life aesthetically, so their art was not detached from their lives as it is today. Similarly, their so-called religion was undetached from their lives as today. Even their social institutions were tied up with their aesthetics. They could not conceive of the disconnect you describe."

"OK but that was then, and this is now." Dorian pursued the relevant.

Azar insisted on the backstory. "It's important to know how we got where we are to be clear about the present. As with everything, the meaning of things which includes words changes with time. Art and beauty are supreme examples. The modern view essentially took its cue from a bogus science of sociology and history. For example, the theory universally adopted was that cavemen drew on walls to represent their environment and tell a story about their culture. But the theory is highly speculative. We can't really see that far back. Rather, it is ancient Greece that provides concrete evidence for humanity's early understanding of art and beauty. And it is decidedly not representation."

Dorian interrupted. "I'm fascinated by Socrates and Plato, so will you say more?" But his deeper interest was in making time with this dark beauty, and he felt he was gaining ground. Azar was fine with that, and regardless she fully intended to spell it all out for him.

"In the Heroic Age art was ritual, that is it was included in what constituted Greek religion. Which is to say, it was the opposite of representation in the modern sense. In as much as the modern theory of art as representation relies on the conceptual division of the object being depicted and the artwork itself, that is the assumption that the subject and object are not the same, the ancient Greeks could never speak of religious representation.

"Now please understand, Dorian, that I do not mean by that that the Greeks did *not* create the gods. They certainly did. But while the poetic epics of Greece brought the gods to experience, which is to say made them up, they were never fictitious. Rather, they emerged from the very life of Greek society and culture itself in its ethical character. This we know to be the case because the Greeks had not yet sought to understand nature and the unseen world of spirit as separate. Again, it is all part of the Heroic Age before the rise of Neoplatonism and subsequently Christianity. In effect, the earlier Greeks did not separate meaning from configuration. Hence, it is correct to say that when the Greek looked at the statue of Aphrodite it was the goddess. But keep in mind, this was true in an idiosyncratic way. The Greek did not believe the statue contained the goddess, which is the perverse modern take on their understanding. But neither did the statue represent Aphrodite, which is the modern abstraction of meaning and form, and in some quarters it still persists. The ancient view was that the statue presents Aphrodite. It is a showing-forth or illuminating of the goddess in a sensuous medium."

"Wait, is this all part of Socrates's fixation with beauty?" Dorian knew of the Platonic quest.

"Precisely because it was from this that the Greeks derived their idea of beauty. But now this is the earlier understanding, the understanding that when the experience of presentation successfully unites nature and spirit, or more philosophically, configuration and meaning, intuition and concept, there is beauty."

Dorian was becoming lost. "Could you simplify that for me?"

"Sure. It can be summarized as harmony, the recognition of beauty when nature is regarded as divine, not apart from its actual people, animals, and the social structures of a culture, but within these people, creatures, and structures. The thing to keep in mind is that law in ancient Greece came about by custom. The law was simply precedent, and generally obeyed because it had always been that way. With the rise of Rome, what emerged in the climate of Rome's imperialism and its dictatorial character was law divorced from nature or what the Greeks had simply assumed was the natural way of things. With Rome governing by law replaced governing by custom. Christianity grew up in this climate, and as a result, the character of that epoch of Christianity became one of severity. Obedience to Rome would run parallel with obedience to the church, and the authority of the church was not to be questioned. Art as a handmaiden of the church was tasked with instruction; to teach the Christian faith by depicting the Christ phenomenon as a historic fact.

"The core of that teaching was Christ's reconciliation of God with humanity. But by doing so nature was treated as ancillary, a mere stage for the reunion of the finite with the infinite. This paved the way for the turn toward subjectivity, and it played out dramatically in the much later development of the modern understanding of art. Ultimately and leading up to the late modern and postmodern periods, art ceased to be formative and the means by which people were integrated into society. Artistic subjectivity led to the autonomy of art and artists, the ultimate cancellation of the classical ideal. Nature was emptied of the gods, and so the world was essentially disenchanted. Progress!"

Dorian thought he followed her track. "And what of spirit?"

"Spirit, my new friend, was banished from nature only to be discovered within oneself."

"New friend," he thought. "This is going well."

Azar continued, "Thus, spirit became unrepresentable—it became infinite freedom moored in the mundane and with that freedom, infinite subjectivity became the infinity of subjective caprice. Art as illusion."

"You know, I think you are giving too much over to ancient Greece," Dorian politely objected not to strain the budding relationship. "You treat it like it was Utopia. But slavery was at the center of their civilization and the misery that entails."

"True enough, but the Greeks recognized that."

"Recognized what? That only some were free? And that was OK, that was natural?"

"Dorian, freedom is not natural."

"The hell it's not." Dorian was feeling patronized by the repetition of his name.

"Dorian, freedom is just another idea. And it was the Greeks that first became conscious of it. Still, they recognized that only some are free, not humanity as such. They accepted that, and allowed the institution of slavery to undergird their glorious experience of liberty."

"That's bullshit."

"Have it your way."

"If one person is not free, no one is free."

"Dorian, how naive." Again, he sensed her patronizing him.

"Where did you get this?" Dorian found it all interesting but incredible.

"Hegel. Georg Wilhelm Frederick Hegel to be precise."

"But he's been dismissed as a credible philosopher."

"Not entirely. Yes, many of his ideas are garbage. But there is much in his thinking to be admired."

Dorian remained unconvinced. "Let's move on, because it seems to me you have told me how we got to where we are in our theory of art, à la Herr Hegel, but we haven't talked about what art is today."

She was glad to accommodate him. "Where Hegel was at his worst was in his belief in the Absolute, that we can think the Absolute, the infinite. We cannot."

"Hell no, we can't."

"And if that is the case, and I can see you agree with me, then it is as you say, art is illusion, form and color. And the chief or only aim of a work of art is the self-expression of the individual artist who creates it. The effect of better art is its ability to capture the imagination, stimulate the mind, change our course, introduce us to a new way of thinking, and possibly produce in us the bliss of ecstasy."

"Right on!" Dorian felt reassured. "So why all this history, all this dredging up the moldy remains of Hegel?"

"To establish our mutual beachhead. No more will we be led down the primrose path. True art must remain divorced from any didactic, moral, political, or utilitarian function."

Dorian was animated. "Whose to doubt it?" Had she won him over, or was she simply confirming her disciple?

"Your hero, Richard Rorty, well he's stepped off the cliff since his stable analytical days."

"He's not my hero. I've read him so I suppose I understand him a little. I like his brutal honesty about pointless talk about what this exhibit is about, the hereafter. And by the way, how do you know I've followed the work of Rorty?"

"You said you were an amateur philosopher."

"Wait, I said that? I must have forgot."

"Rorty has unwittingly created a metaphysical loophole with his late utopianism that needs to be closed."

"What's that?"

"He's left room for the do-gooders. His negative argumentation, perhaps unintentionally, leaks the numinous. It's one thing to stand behind private irony and quite another to suggest a tension there with liberal hope. His musings about aesthetic bliss are deceptive because they cannot be reconciled with his view of social activism. You serve mammon or you're doomed to a life of anachronism serving God."

Dorian mused to himself, "Where have I heard that before?" Now aloud, "But how does that connect with modern art?"

"Art must remain art for art's sake. Aesthetic values alone should guide their operations. Art is the repository of human culture, and art museums play a major role in advancing the Enlightenment's idea that the display of art for everyone's edification allows us to better understand the world. For that to happen art must remain neutral. It fails when it moves from pure aesthetic interest to teaching lessons: to social activism, forcing the taking of sides on issues like fascism rather than remaining concretely harbored in the pure aestheticism that befits it."

"Ya, Rorty is as slippery as a fish, all right. But he's not my hero, just another philosopher."

"Good. I can see you are keeping to your common sense."

"You seem to know a lot about me for someone I just met."

"I can just tell it from our conversation."

"Your lecture you mean," he chuckled so as not to offend her. "She's a regular Madame Boob-ary," he quipped not daring to say it out loud. Still, he couldn't resist smiling thinking he was so very witty.

"What's so funny?"

"Nothing," Dorian remained evasive.

Azar wasn't quite finished. She insisted on drawing a parallel between art and life and culture. "Do you know anything about queer theory?"

"Please don't tell me you're a lesbian," Dorian implored.

"What's it to you?" Azar scolded. "Besides, here I'm not talking about sexual identity, not specifically."

"Good," Dorian felt relieved.

"It is an approach to understanding our affections. It provides a useful alternative to philosophy's obsession with language. It gets beyond language to the actual things that make bodies move, that is act in certain, sometimes contradictory, ways. With its understanding of desire, it reveals the strangeness of our experience, its inscrutability. It puts up a strong argument against the dominance of the older theory that our emotions are purely the product of discursive social construction. That we resolve issues through analytical reasoning. The fact of the matter is language is not so mechanistic. It's not some computer program that compels our movement, our decisions, our desires."

Azar continued, "Also, queer theory revealed subjects who in many ways are governed by forces that are beyond their power to resist, or are such that they cannot simply be dismissed by an act of will, an appeal to conscience or religious dogma."

"But what makes you so sure?" Once again Dorian was lured into a conversation in which he might have to think.

"Well, we see it so clearly as for example with falling in love—we do not choose that person, nor can we really know what it is that brings love about. Same with grief. We lose someone we love, but we cannot determine how painful, how deeply distraught we will be, or how long we will suffer. These are beyond our control. Addiction is another example. Most often we don't want it, but we are powerless to overcome it. Same with some of our deepest political convictions."

"Of course!" Dorian was excited. "That explains a great deal. We are subject to these forces. So, in a sense, they make us who we are, and we are powerless to resist."

"Ah, you are coming round to a clear understanding of human behavior then, Dorian. It has been proven by psychiatric science that when we don't get what we want we get sick."

"Yes, this is making things so very clear to me. It simply reaffirms what I have always believed."

Azar smiled. "You mean felt."

Dorian smiled back at her smug smile. "Right, of course, we are what we feel and that's the gist of it. Why be troubled by guilt? Why question behaviors that emerge from deep within, behaviors that we are powerless to resist?"

Azar's eyes tightened to slits of black and her lips pursed to evoke a kissing motion. Then she smiled ever so slightly, more a grin of satisfaction.

"But Kelly," Dorian felt he could further their intimacy, "could this backfire? If art remains politically neutral isn't it possible that the herd will look to be led by a possibly insidious source of inspiration? Ideologues will make a case that neutrality in art is a hoax, a way of legitimizing old structures of power?"

"Yes, Dorian, isn't it delicious? The battle over art will intensify the chaos and divide people more than ever." Kelly was staring away, off somewhere, Dorian did not know where. And on her face was the same wry grin he noticed as she studied Bosch.

"Listen, Kelly, this is so interesting, but I got to go. Still, I'd like to continue our conversation. How about dinner? Can I take you to a favorite of mine, the 21 Club?"

Located at 21 West Fifty-Second Street, 21 Club was a former speakeasy grown into one of the finest restaurants in the world. It boasted a cellar of forty thousand bottles and a menu of fine and imaginative signature recipes. Dorian was making his own efforts at temptation. "If you haven't been there you'll be impressed by the outstanding art collection. You can view Remington, Barclay, and

Crandall in the most eclectic setting you can imagine. I'll come by with a cab tonight and pick you up. Where do you live?"

"I'll tell you what, how about we rendezvous there at say, nine o'clock tonight? Can you manage a reservation at this late date?"

"Believe me, I get in whenever I want."

"OK, it's a date. I'll see you there."

"See you there."

Dorian was determined *not* to continue the conversation but to lure her away, to let her tell him her life's story so he could sympathize, win her over, and seduce her. When he left his apartment he was filled with lofty expectations. He felt he had laid all the necessary groundwork, and now all that remained was the gentle persuasion that would convince her that he was her soul mate.

He arrived at 21 Club just a few minutes early, paid the cab driver, and made his way to the beautiful golden entryway being guarded by a calvary of ornamental jockeys. He strode expectantly past the barroom with its iconic toy collection hanging from the ceiling including a baseball bat used by Willie Mays and was met by Michael the maître d' who seated him at his usual table. A friendly and familiar waiter, Hector, rushed over to him and greeted him like an old pal. Dorian said he was waiting for his date and ordered a Lagavulin on the rocks. It was gone in fifteen minutes with no Kelly in sight. He ordered a second which he nursed for thirty minutes.

That gone, Hector came over with a sympathetic look on his face. "Mr. Fist, can I get you something for dinner? It's getting late and the kitchen is about to close."

"No, Hector, I guess I'm not hungry. Just get me another Scotch and the check." Dorian was furious but not appearing so. "This isn't happening," Dorian fumed to himself. "Unacceptable. I can't believe it. Never has this happened. Who the hell does she think she is?"

Hector brought the scotch and the check. "Thanks, Hector. Hey, call me a cab will you?" Instead of his usual slow but steady sipping, Dorian threw back the Scotch and realized this was a Manhattan restaurant glass of scotch. It would have to be taken in doses. Two large swallows more and he got up from the table. Less in control than he would like he slammed the chair against the table. "Bitch," he blurted out, evoking curious stares and a few scolding frowns from the flustered patrons.

After another silent cab ride home, feeling miserable and disgraced, Dorian decided this was it now. Never again. "After all, what's to be gained?" He didn't sleep that night. The following weekend, on Sunday, he called a number he had gotten from a sales rep from Volkswagen for whom he was doing consulting work on the side without telling anybody.

Lianne Lu was a concierge at Manhattan's famous Plaza Hotel. "Hi, this is Dorian Fist. Mark Bellarmine gave me your number and said you were discreet and could be trusted. I'm looking for a date."

"Mr. Fist I don't know any Mark Bellarmine, and I'm not a dating service." She had only the slightest hint of an accent, Mandarin, or some dialect of it, he reasoned.

"That's not what I was told," Dorian remained polite.

"Well, you were told wrong, goodbye," she hung up on him.

Ten minutes later his phone rang. "Dorian Fist," he answered.

"Mr. Fist, this is Lianne Lu. We spoke a few minutes ago."

"Yes, of course, what can I do for you?"

"I'm sure you understand the importance of discretion and privacy here. It was necessary that I speak to Mr. Bellarmine. He's a good and trusted customer and he vouched for you."

"Great, so do I get that date?" Dorian was eager.

"Depends. First is the fee. Our girls are high-end, handpicked by us, and carefully monitored. We accept no funny business on either end. Any harm comes to one of them and you will likely not see the morning. Understood?"

"Without question."

Lianne went on, "So, the fee is $10,000 a night, or $2,500 an hour."

Dorian was fine with that. "Perfect, book me a room at the Plaza for this Friday night. Tell her she will be there about two hours. Say, starting around 10 p.m."

"Agreed, Mr. Fist. But we need to find you the right girl. I'm going to send you a link. It will appear to be nothing other than a website for models who are looking for work. If a box appears by her picture she is free for the evening and at the time you requested. Check the box and that will be your date. Also, you will need to text me your picture at this number so that your date will be able to recognize you. Come to the concierge desk at the Plaza at about quarter to ten on Friday night. I will meet you there, check you in, get you your room key, and send you to our Palm Court Bar. Your date will want to confirm that it is you and that she feels comfortable. Then she will join you. Buy her a drink and you're off to the races. Keep in mind you have two hours." It was a well-rehearsed script.

Lianne Lu was wrapping up. "I will need you to send me the amount in full, five thousand dollars, twenty-four hours before your date. You can use PayPal or something similar—we use most of these services. If for any acceptable reason the date does not take place, your money will be refunded in full. We are an honest business with an impeccable reputation, and we treat our customers well. How does all this sound?"

"Fine."

"Nice doing business with you, Mr. Fist. Oh, and don't forget that picture. See you Friday."

"See you Friday."

They both hung up.

"Perfect," Dorian decided. "No pointless pursuit, no making believe I care, no drama, and no worthless conversation."

Monday he was back at work and reasonably back together. At 11 a.m. Dorian got a call on his personal cell phone. The conversation was in German. Volkswagen wanted him in Wolfsburg, Germany, ASAP. Once off the phone, he put in a request to HR for a two-week vacation. He got a call back in minutes. It was a casual friend and colleague named Pete Richards. They had golfed together once or twice and were part of a foursome in an annual charity tournament. "Dorian, you ok?"

"Ya, why?"

"Bro, in the nine years you've been with Carriage, you never once asked for vacation time. So, it's a bit of a mystery. But hell ya, knock yourself out, have a good time and enjoy it. You've earned it. When you want off?"

"Can I get next week for two weeks then?"

"Are you sure there's nothing wrong? But hey, that's your business. You got it. See ya when you get back. Peace."

Friday night he met Lianne Lu at the concierge desk. She checked him in and sent him to the Palm Court Bar. He ordered his Lagavulin from Richie the bartender who was annoyingly friendly. In a few minutes, he noticed a beautiful woman seated in a dark corner of the bar glancing down at a picture and up at him. She paused, smiled, and walked seductively toward him, taking the barstool next to him. She looked exactly like her picture, stunning and elegantly coiffured. Her hair was blond, and Dorian fantasized she was German. She wore a blue Monique Lhuillier rhinestone chain mail evening gown, slit at the left leg to the top of her slender thigh. The gown was cut low accentuating her breasts, with thin straps leading up to her shoulders and down her back.

"Mr. Fist, I'm Elsa," she spoke with just the slightest German accent.

"Bingo," Dorian whispered. Now out loud, "*Was trinkst du?*" Dorian's German was impeccable. "Oh, and call me Dorian."

"Champaign—Richie, get me my usual will you darling? So, you are German or at least you speak it well?" The bartender smiled and brought her a flute alive with the tiny white bubbles so admired by those who adore champaign.

They drank in silence, and when he saw her glass was empty he said, "Richie, put that on room 333 and tag on 25 percent for yourself. Oh, and thanks." Then to Elsa, "*Sollen wir gehen?*"

"Of course," Elsa complied. Not another word was uttered until at twelve midnight, she got up from the bed and got dressed. He said goodbye and she responded in kind.

For Dorian it was as if his soul, if he had one, was outside himself, watching from the settee. The man in the bed with the model was an actor in a steamy movie without a plot. Not even

95

good pornography. Elsa wasn't a bad actor, but acting was all it was. And the man was really a little boy, doing what his hormones dictated, looking for his mother in this fictitious woman; needing to be loved but not allowing it; subjugating any idea of love to passion, and allowing passion to determine the course of the next two hours. That Elsa was not his nor ever would be made her the perfect substitute. That way he could indulge himself without feeling seedy, without any hint of incest, in his warped view of things. Hollow yet sexually satisfied, the role would have to do. The role was all that Dorian would allow himself. The role was something he could walk away from in the morning and play again when he needed to. And he would over and over again.

Back at Carriage on Monday he booked his flight for the next Monday out of JFK and flew nonstop to Hannover. From there he took a train to Wolfsburg. He met Bernard Dosé, chief engineer for Volkswagen, over lunch. "We received the software you designed, Mr. Fist, but we wanted you here when we entered the code in the engine control unit. We're still working out the bugs, but it shouldn't be long until we can begin rigging the tests."

"Call me Dorian." He was pleased with their progress. "Good, that unit will detect when emission tests are being performed, and it will change the way the engine runs."

"Right," Dosé confirmed, "we understand that."

"Make sure the tests are done on a rolling road so that the car is stationary. That way you can control the test conditions. Also, see to it that every car is tested in the same manner. The code will alter the timing of the engine to reduce fuel efficiency and reduce emissions. In that mode, it will produce lower nitrogen oxides."

Dosé was ticking off his checklist. "As I understand it the car thinks it's driving in a normal manner?"

"Not precisely. It's the ECU when it's running that *thinks* it's driving. The steering wheel must be altered such that it never turns more than fifteen degrees. That way the car will switch to low emissions mode and cheat the test."

"So, it's not really real-world driving is it?"

"Not at all, and that's the key. In real-world driving you don't turn the ignition and drive in a perfectly straight line. Rather, with the wheel turning in a normal manner the ECU will increase the power which gives better fuel economy, but it produces higher levels of NOx. Believe me, it's foolproof."

The next day Dorian met with some engineers at the Wolfsburg plant, they went over the specs again and decided they were ready to move the scheme forward. Dorian was essentially done there. Bored, he changed his ticket and got an early flight back to the states. Pete came by his office the next day and asked what he was doing there.

"I was bored."

"Just like you," Pete laughed as he left the office.

The news didn't break about the fix until 2014. It all came to light when some people were trying to replicate the tests but doing it in the real world with portable equipment on the car, instead of in a test facility. They found that the results were wildly different from the manufacturer's published test figures. But by then Dorian had hacked Volkswagen's computers and wiped them clean of any mention of him or his work. His name never came up in the scandal.

A few years after his return from Wolfsburg and back hard at work, Dorian got a call from a lawyer telling him that Connie Matthews was suing him for sexual assault, in this case, rape. He said that his client was willing to settle for a single cash payout. Dorian was livid and slammed the phone down. He called his lawyer and made an appointment. He met Phillip Dunbarton in his office the following week and gave a complete rundown of their relationship and breakup. Dunbarton recommended he just settle as long as it was not extortionate. Dorian stubbornly refused. "This is bullshit, and it's wrong, and I'm not laying down. The woman is a demon."

When the case came to trial, Dorian's lawyer invested everything he had in the testimony of Ryerson Erden, along with the fact that there was no evidence that Connie Matthews had sought help or filed a complaint. Still, he called as witnesses several Carriage people familiar with Connie and Dorian, each one testifying that they never saw any sign of conflict and no hint of violence. But the case would come down to the testimony of Erden.

"How often did you observe Mr. Fist and Ms. Matthews together?" Dunbarton asked.

Erden answered, "A dozen times or so. Right up until the incident with the car? Yep, up until that very day."

"Mr. Erden, did you notice anything out of order in their relationship before the day Ms. Matthews drove the Porsche?"

"Objection." Connie's lawyer said Dunbarton was leading the witness.

"Your honor, how are we going to establish whether Ms. Matthews was really raped without knowing anything about their relationship? We have no call to 911, no police report, no visit to a hospital. There are no individuals willing to testify that she spoke to them of this. Nothing. So, we need to discover if she outwardly showed any emotional or physical distress at any time with regard to my client."

"Objection overruled." The judge obliged, "Answer the question, Mr. Erden."

"No, they seemed fine together."

Dunbarton continued, "Was Ms. Matthews ever seen leaving the building in an agitated state?"

"No and security would have informed me if that were the case. The owners of the building want absolutely no public embarrassment."

"Mr. Erden, what in your estimation were Mr. Fist's feelings about his car?"

"Objection."

"Your honor, I am just trying to establish the degree of Mr. Fist's fondness for his automobile. As this has nothing to do with the question of rape, why would learned counsel object to this line of questioning?"

"Overruled." Again, "Mr. Erden just answer the question."

"He adorned it. He almost worshiped it."

"So, Mr. Erden, when Mr. Fist was told that Ms. Matthews had taken his car what was his reaction?"

"He went crazy at me. Told me she was a bald-faced liar."

"How long after her return did you no longer see her in the building?"

"Immediately. Immediately after that, Mr. Fist said she was never permitted in the building again."

"In your judgment was the car incident the reason for the breakup?"

"Objection. Your honor that calls for the conclusion of the witness."

"Sustained."

Counsel for the defense redirected his line of questioning. "Ok, then let's just stick to the facts. You gave Ms. Matthews the keys to the Porsche without Mr. Fist's permission. Is that correct?"

"It is."

"And when Mr. Fist confronted you about that what did he say?"

"Mr. Fist was all over me for letting her have the keys. He said she was a cold-blooded liar, and he never wanted to see her again."

"Was Ms. Matthews ever seen in the building again according to your security people?"

"No."

"So, in your estimation, was the stolen car the reason for Ms. Matthews bringing charges against Mr. Fist?"

"Objection. Your honor, my client is not on trial here."

"Sustained."

"Ok, Mr. Erden, did Mr. Fist tell you outright that he would never see Ms. Matthews again, and that it was because of the incident with the car?"

"Yes."

The jury returned a verdict of not guilty. Once again, cat-like, Dorian landed on his feet. Pete in HR said he must have nine lives, but Dorian was unmoved by the whole drama. In fact, he could care less other than to get back at Connie whatever the cost. He felt betrayed. In every visible way, Dorian was unchanged. But about a year later and back at work with a vengeance, he began to experience stomach pain. At first, it was simply heartburn and occasionally acid regurgitation. He started swallowing antacids by the handful and overmedicating with Tylenol. He thought maybe he was just working too hard, but he had no intention of slowing down—the pace devoured his memories. Pete told him that he probably had an ulcer, so he had it checked out. No ulcer.

In a few months, the symptoms intensified, and he began to experience frequent nausea that would lead to spells of vomiting. He rarely finished a meal, became full even when he had little to eat, and his chest felt like it would explode. He began to lose a lot of weight, on a body that was not the least overweight. Food became an issue, and he had trouble with digestion. The problem became so severe he thought he might die. He made another appointment with his doctor, Aldert VanderKooi, who ordered every test in the book relating to Dorian's condition. Nothing.

After the last test result came back negative, VanderKooi personally called him to ask him to come in for a consultation. Dorian thought maybe the doctor had come up with a diagnosis and hopefully a treatment. However, when he arrived at the doctor's office the physician had a worried look on his face that rattled Dorian. He shook his head and said, "Dorian you're a bit of a mystery. Your symptoms are as you say. We're seeing early satiety, postprandial fullness, and bloating in the upper abdomen. Given all the negative tests, I've come to the conclusion that you have nonulcerdyspepsiais. It's the only diagnosis that makes sense."

"Nonulcer what in the world?" Dorian babbled.

"Nonulcerdyspepsiais. It's as hard to pronounce as to pin down." VanderKooi laughed, but Dorian didn't find it funny at all.

VanderKooi continued more grimly. "It used to be called dyspepsia. It still is by many. That's its more common name."

"What the hell is it? Am I dying? Is it contagious?"

"No, Dorian none of those things. The thing about dyspepsia is that it's extremely unlikely that you will die from it. Nor do the symptoms have any structural or biochemical explanation."

"So, what's the cure?"

"Well, that's the problem. As I said there is no scientific explanation. Some studies suggest that anxiety and emotional distress may play a part."

"I don't have any of that," Dorian was adamant. "Hey, wait, are you suggesting this is psychological, that it's somehow psychosomatic?"

"Well, that's what we think with dyspepsia. We've seen some success in treatment with antidepressants, and I can set you up with that."

"But I'm not depressed. Doc you got to believe me. This isn't in my head. This is some kind of bug. This is something physiological, not psychological."

"Dorian you can certainly seek another opinion, but maybe you should consult with a psychologist or psychiatrist first to see what might be there."

"There's nothing there."

"Just my advice. As far as a biomedical approach, I have nothing for you other than Remeron or Ludiomil or the like. We can see what works best for you."

"Hell, no Doc. I'm telling you this thing is an attack from the outside, from who knows what. It's not in my head."

"Sorry Dorian, that's all I've got for you."

Dorian was convinced that what ailed him was physiological. But after another battery of tests and several consultations with another highly respected physician, the result was the same. Dyspepsia.

Dorian was falling apart. In his entire life, he could not remember being sick other than an occasional cold. Now he could barely function, and it weighed on his mind. He became morose and started missing work. He began scouring the internet for experimental treatments, but none of them really addressed the problem. Then he stumbled on a website from a "hospital" in Montego Bay, Jamaica. A doctor there, Milano DeSantos, claimed to have discovered an herbal medicine that was "100 percent effective in curing stomach related illness such as gastroenteritis, gastritis, and dyspepsia." Dorian was desperate. The site detailed DeSantos's research into a plant called bissy, or *Cola acuminata*, found in the lowland forests of Jamaica and used for generations by the people who lived there. The website described how DeSantos's experiments led to the discovery that the "miraculous benefits" of the plant's active ingredients, theobromine and kolatin, were only fully realized when combined with a regiment of very specific vitamins and nutrients. The blended ingredients, the base of which were theobromine, tannins, flavonoids, and caffeine, were then synthesized into a serum, all of which was exclusive to DeSantos's hospital. The synthesized serum allegedly cured stomach issues while boosting the immune system without side effects.

Dorian dialed the number on the website. "Dr. DeSantos, please."

"Dr. DeSantos is with a patient at the moment. Do you care to wait, or would you like him to return your call?" The lilting Jamaican accent was like a tropical breeze, conjuring up images of palm trees and coconuts, steel bands and rum drinks. Not to the distraught Dorian. "How long will it be?"

"Perhaps thirty minutes or so. I can always have the doctor call you back."

"No, I'll wait." Dorian could not wait. He put the phone on speaker and began to pace. It was all of thirty minutes when the doctor took the phone.

"Dr. DeSantos," Dorian was met with the same melodic accent. It fell on deaf ears. Dorian laid out his misery in excruciating detail.

"Dyspepsia," the doctor returned.

"Ya, I guess. Can you do anything for me?"

"I have several pages of personal testimonies as to the effectiveness of my treatment. Perhaps you've checked the website, but there are pages more if you are interested?"

"Yes I have, and no I'm not," came back the impatient patient. Dorian knew all about the manufacture of personal testimonies, but his despair made any gamble worth the trouble. "When can you see me?"

"When can you come to the island?"

"Well, let's see, this is Wednesday. I think I can get a nonstop to Montego Bay at 9:00 a.m. on Friday. It's a little more than a three-hour flight. With any luck, I can be in your office by the early afternoon. Does that work?"

DeStantos felt he needed to talk about money first. "Do you want to talk about treatment costs?"

"I don't care what it costs if it works." Ordinarily Dorian would not be so carefree with his money, but his suffering and state of mind had him acting recklessly. "We can discuss what this will cost when I get there. As long as everything is above board and reasonable we will have no issues."

"Of course, I fully agree," the doctor was satisfied. "And you will be delighted with the results, I assure you."

"Fine. I will see you then on Friday afternoon at your hospital."

There was a slight pause, after which the doctor corrected, "Perhaps you should say clinic."

"But your website?"

"That is the familiar term to us Jamaicans. You Americans, I'm sure, would prefer the term clinic in this case."

"Fine, clinic. Friday afternoon. See you then." No red lights appeared in Dorian's rearview. He was too sick, too miserable. The doctor was concluding, "Please wait on the line for my receptionist to get all the necessary medical information, your background and history, and a payment plan. If we do that now we can go straight away into treatment when you get here. Is that acceptable, Mr. Fist?"

"It's fine. I'll hang on and see you Friday."

"I will see you Friday and safe travels."

Dorian provided the information asked of him by the receptionist. Hanging up, he went straight to the bathroom and threw up. He no longer paused at mirrors but virtually ran to the toilet. Miserable he filled a tall glass of scotch, drank it, and went to bed. He had wild nightmares. He dreamed he was floating on a cloud and a crow came sailing by. "Crow," he said, "how high up are we?"

"I'm a raven, not a crow," the bird sounded indignant.

Dorian shot back, "Ridiculous! A raven's just a big crow. You are both of the family *Corvidae*, and *Corvus* of the same genus. Like I said, you're just a big crow. How high up are we?"

"Ah, but we are our own species. Size is only one thing. And why not say that crows are just small ravens?"

"I'm sure I will fall, and I need to know how far that will be."

"Look again at my beak and you will never again call me a crow."

"Are there other clouds nearby and below me, clouds that I can jump to and make my way down? Can you circle around and scout them out?"

The raven ignored him. "And look at the plumage around my neck. It's like a mantle, the sign of royalty. That is why some call me Waldram."

"Are you willing to help me? I really am desperate."

"Are you willing to concede the point?"

"What point?"

"That I am not a big crow."

"Yes anything, anything if you can help me get down."

"But you don't really believe it do you?"

"If it satisfies you I will believe anything you say if you will just help me."

"You must believe it in your heart."

"You're not a crow or a raven, you're a looney bird. So, fuck off."

"You are no more than three feet off the ground, but no matter, the fall will kill you." With that, it stretched its enormous wings and soared toward the sun, a sun that suddenly looked exactly like the tunnel of light in Bosch's painting *Ascent to Heaven*. The raven began to glow, its wings turning white, and its body becoming that of a boy or a woman in flowing robes.

Dorian woke shaking and sweating. The bed was soaked, he had a terrible feeling of pressure in his chest, and he made for the toilet. He spent the night huddled over it, and each time he tried to make his way back to bed he would turn back to the toilet. He would nod there, momentarily adrift, dream chaotic dreams, and then wake and vomit. He longed to be on his way to Jamaica.

7

MONTEGO BAY, JAMAICA, 2017

O N Friday Dorian Fist caught a cab to JFK and from there flew straight to Montego Bay. He caught another cab from the Sangster International Airport in St. James to the Tallyman Hotel, a short twenty-minute commute. The Tallyman was no showpiece, nor was Dorian interested in elegance or comfort. It was, however, a brief drive from Church Street, which was the main drag downtown where the clinic was located. He checked in and saw he was due at the clinic in an hour. He tried to rest, but felt nauseous and couldn't sleep. As the hour wore on he went to the hotel desk and had them call him a cab. It was just a quick hop to his destination. He could have walked, but he was too ill.

The roads were crowded with cars, buses, scooters, and bicycles, most decades old. Without street lines the traffic seemed to flow dangerously in and out. The sky was as blue as the nearby bay the town was named for, and a sea breeze made the eighty-five-degree temperature feel utterly pleasant. Dorian looked haplessly out the window as he neared his destination. The curbs were painted yellow with blue pedestrian fences on the main corners. The shops were also brightly painted, most with equally bright awnings. The sidewalk was filled with locals and tourists.

The cab pulled up to the address supplied by Dorian. The "hospital" was by no means a hospital, and if it was a clinic it was only so in name. It was a storefront, not even on the first floor. Dorian had to navigate his way through the tobacco store on the first floor specializing in Cuban cigars. Also on offer was another popular smoke. "Spliff, mon?" came an offer from behind the counter. Dorian never took his eyes off the staircase leading to the "clinic." He was met there by the receptionist whose voice he recognized.

"Mr. Fist?" she asked.

"Yes."

"Please, the doctor is waiting for you, go right in."

By now the series of tests were all too familiar to Dorian, and he was utterly frustrated. Still, his impatience couldn't rattle the staff whose cherry island dispositions seemed beyond all unnerving. They spoke patois to each other, but knowing Dorian would not understand they switched to English when addressing him. Both languages rang songlike and lilting in the islanders' pronunciation. However, there were words that he couldn't understand. The head nurse, Amoy, confronted Dorian's impatience with a stern "cuse mi please, bill," which he later learned meant "relax."

Tests completed the doctor was satisfied that Dorian had dyspepsia, and he outlined the treatment. "The serum is to be taken by the mouth in the morning and evening. I want you to stay in Jamaica for a week so I can observe you. By then you should be well on your way to mending. You'll be taking the serum for a month at home after that to make sure you're completely cured. Is that clear?"

Dorian asked him, "Do I come to the clinic for the serum during the first week?"

"Yes, but only in the morning, and I will check you out to make sure all is going well. At the end of the week, you will be fine and headed home again." That completed, the doctor said, "Manners an' respect."

"Sorry?" Dorian didn't understand.

"Oh, yes, of course," the doctor smiled. "See you later."

Monday and Tuesday Dorian lay in bed most of the day and evening except when making his daily trip to the clinic. On

Wednesday he woke in the early morning after a good night's sleep, something he hadn't had in months. He felt well enough to venture into Montego Bay to do a little sightseeing. That evening he even risked a jerk chicken with pigeon peas and rice. He ate everything on his plate. More importantly, he kept it down. As for drink, he settled for rum not recognizing any of the scotches on offer. He decided to walk home and enjoy the beautiful Caribbean evening, with soft tropical breezes moving the palms in time with the reggae music wafting from the open doors of every bar and restaurant on Church Street. Once again he slept through the night.

It was as the doctor had said and by Thursday he felt much better. He booked a one-way flight back to JFK on Saturday. He felt as if he had licked the devil himself and laughed at the great doctors of New York City who thought everything he suffered from was in his head. He actually began to doze once in the air, but early in the flight he suddenly woke with a start. His chest was about to explode, and a wave of nausea overwhelmed him. In spite of the seat belt sign being on, he unbuckled himself and made an urgent dash for the bathroom. Before the attendant could come on the intercom to reprimand him he collapsed in the aisle and knew nothing again until he woke up in a hospital room.

8

MIAMI BEACH, FLORIDA, 2017

THE plane had been diverted to Miami Beach, and an ambulance took Dorian to Jackson Memorial Hospital. Coming to he peered around the room and realized he wasn't in ER, that was obvious, but he was on an IV. "You were badly dehydrated Mr. Fist," said a nurse, noticing he was awake, making her way to his bed. "Dehydrated and malnourished. We did a series of tests but came up with nothing. Is there a condition that you suffer from that you are aware of?"

"They tell me I have dyspepsia, but I don't believe them. This is some kind of mysterious disease."

"Well, we couldn't find anything. You're too weak to travel, and so we are making arrangements for a rehab facility where you can regain your strength."

"You aren't planning on condemning me to a nursing home, are you? That ain't gonna happen."

"No Mr. Fist, just a temporary stay at rehab should put you right."

"Well, OK, but as soon as I regain my strength and get on a plane, I'll be outa here."

"Of course, Mr. Fist, but the doctors will have to sign you out."

"We'll see about that."

The next day an ambulance transported Dorian to Ravenswood Rehabilitation and Long-Term Care Center in Downtown Miami. As the EMS technician wheeled him into the facility he noticed that several of the patients lined the halls typically in wheelchairs. Two elderly ladies seemed to brighten as he rolled past them. "He's so young," they tittered. "Why do you suppose he's here? I read on the patient register he's Dorian Fist. So cute. Hi Dorian," they flirted and giggled.

Instead of being delighted, the attention devastated Dorian. But the irony was lost on him. The one most desirous of attention was in a place where he was the youngest looking outside of the staff and among the youngest in age as well, someone sure to be popular and sought after, and yet it galled him and drove him to deep despair.

Two weeks passed and Dorian was no better. He could barely eat, and his strength seemed to be ebbing for no medical reason. Doctors came and went without a hint of a prognosis. "You're a real mystery, Mr. Fist," a young and tanned Hispanic physician teased him. It made Dorian hate him, and he requested that the doctor no longer be assigned to him.

"Sorry Mr. Fist," the attending nurse replied, "that is something you have no say about." Caged and powerless his depression intensified. With no sign of recovery and no prospect of returning home, he began to wish he were dead. A month had passed, and it was early morning when he heard a knock at his open door. It was a brown-haired, pleasant-looking woman, perhaps in her middle forties. She had a round and full figure and wore no makeup. No more than five foot four, her shoes were simple flats as if she preferred comfort to style. Her light brown hair neatly tied back in a ponytail shown bright and soft in the morning sun coming through the window. She wore the same gown worn by the Ravenswood staff, blue and drab, clinical looking, with an attached belt circling her ample waist. Still, she was the only one of her colleagues who tied it in a bow in the front rather than the back. Her badge said Sophia Milhaud. "Good morning Mr. Fist, I have your breakfast." She had a charming French accent and an unassuming manner. Her smile was delightful, but Dorian was predisposed to hate everybody and everything.

"I'm not hungry," he grumbled.

"OK, but I know you want to get your strength back. I'll just leave it for you." She wasn't pushy like some of the other staff. "Oh, and I brought you something you might like. It's the New York Times. I saw that you are from New York City, and I thought you might be missing your paper by now."

He never read newspapers other than the trade papers, and he had no interest in beginning now. However, this simple act of kindness in his most desperate hour touched him somehow. Yet all he managed was "fine, leave it on the table." He never looked at it again.

The following morning went very much the same, but this time Dorian tried to hold down some toast and eggs. The coffee was rancid and horrible, but for reasons he could not fathom, he said nothing. But neither did he drink it.

"It's horrible swill, isn't it?" Sophia stated more than asked. "Wait." She took out her thermos and poured him a hot cup of cappuccino. "How can people tolerate such a noxious brew?" She laughed, and for the first time in a long while he smiled. Not at the joke. It was her laugh. So real and earnest—as if it were a joke on life itself.

"I can't stay long this morning because there are two new patients being admitted down the hall, but tomorrow I promise I will have something special for you, something besides a decent cup of coffee."

Dorian looked at her astonished. His face was a mask that showed no emotion. His eyes teared ever so slightly at his misery, his misery in light of her kindness. He looked down and said nothing.

"*Au revoir,*" she chirped.

On the third morning, the world changed for Dorian Fist. Sophia arrived in much the same way as before except excited. This time he welcomed the eggs and toast, but more the coffee and company. "Your color is better Mr. Fist," Sophia smiled.

"Call me Dorian." Resistance to this cheerful French woman seemed pointless. "What am I feeling?" he mused.

"While you eat and enjoy your coffee I had promised something special and now it is time. May I read to you?"

"Read what?"

"Oh, just a short poem, this one by William Wordsworth. It's called 'The World Is Too Much With Us.'" Dorian said nothing, and so she took it as a yes. Instead of a chair, she joined him on his bed. In her hand was a worn and ragged leather-bound book. Never taking her eyes off the widow that blazed brightly in the sunlit Miami sky, she recited,

> The world is too much with us; late and soon,
> Getting and spending, we lay waste our powers:
> Little we see in Nature that is ours;
> We have given our hearts away, a sordid boon!
> This Sea that bares her bosom to the moon;
> The winds that will be howling at all hours,
> And are up-gathered now like sleeping flowers;
> For this, for every thing, we are out of tune;
> It moves us not.—Great God! I'd rather be
> A Pagan suckled in a creed outworn;
> So might I, standing on this pleasant lea,
> Have glimpses that would make me less forlorn;
> Have sight of Proteus rising from the sea;
> Or hear old Triton blow his wreathèd horn.

For what seemed a long minute or two, not a word was uttered. At last, Dorian asked, "Why this poem?"

"For the words, 'the world is too much with us; late and soon. Getting and spending, we lay waste our powers.'"

"Ah so, and may I ask what you have gathered like sleeping flowers?" Dorian was curious.

"I have gathered a less forlorn glimpse to put us back on key. Only this. I only see how much this world is with us, and how our hearts are traded for unworthy gain."

"I am not sure what you mean."

"I mean only that I want you to be comfortable because I have to go. Let me tuck you in. You might need a nap after all this commotion. I will see you tomorrow."

"Tomorrow then." Dorian was utterly undone. But he felt a bit less anxious than he had in months. He did nap. For the first time in a long while he rested comfortably without dreaming, his chest and stomach giving him a short reprieve, his breathing less desperate.

When Sophia arrived the next morning she literally bounded up to him and exploded with childish laughter. "Dorian you will never believe. This morning my cat, Pascal, well he had brought me two little potatoes from the kitchen and put them in my bed during the night. When I woke I laughed so hard that Pascal grabbed one of the potatoes and returned it to the kitchen. I think he believed he had misbehaved. I haven't stopped laughing. So, you're looking stronger today, you must have rested well. How do you feel?"

"Same."

"Hmmm, well, this too shall pass. I have your coffee, but the cook decided it would be pancakes this morning. They look to me more like saucers, what you Americans call Frisbees, just as stiff and hard. Why don't you in this country realize the better choice is for crepes? So much lighter, thin, and flavorful."

Her playful prattle strangely eased Dorian's pain. However, he was still tired, and heeding her warning more whispered than said, "I think I'll just settle for the coffee, and perhaps you could read to me."

"You should eat."

"Please just read. Do you have something this morning?"

"Yes, in fact, I do. I'm sure you are familiar with the sonnets of Shakespeare. Here is one I am especially fond of." She hopped up on the bed, seemingly carefree and oblivious to Dorian's personal space, and began to read from another of her worn tomes.

> Let me not to the marriage of true minds
> Admit impediments. Love is not love
> Which alters when it alteration finds,
> Or bends with the remover to remove:

O no! it is an ever-fixed mark
That looks on tempests and is never shaken;
It is the star to every wandering bark,
Whose worth's unknown, although his height be taken.
Love's not Time's fool, though rosy lips and cheeks
Within his bending sickle's compass come:
Love alters not with his brief hours and weeks,
But bears it out even to the edge of doom.
If this be error and upon me proved,
I never writ, nor no man ever loved.

Dorian's countenance turned dark, and what little color he had faded. "I cannot bear your poetry. It incriminates me. But neither can I bear not to hear you read. But don't read to me. Tell me of yourself." Shocking himself, he actually wanted to know.

Sophia looked sadly at Dorian, glanced at the door, and said, "I have little time, but I will give you the short version. I come from Dijon near the River Seine. That's where I was born and grew up. I went to school at the Sorbonne. But when I was in my second year my parents got sick, and I had to work and look after them. They passed away, and I came to America. I worked for a while in a rest home in Homestead, but just recently I got this job at Ravenswood."

"Are you married?"

"No."

"Do you live alone?"

"No. I have Pascal."

"You say you went to the Sorbonne. What did you study there?"

"Philosophy."

Dorian cocked his head and his eyes brightened. "What do you know of philosophy?" he begged. "No, let me ask you first of your fellow countryman, Michele Foucault. What do you make of him?"

Again, Sophia glanced at the door. "I will tell you when next I see you if you still wish to know. But for now, I must go. Try and rest and regain your strength. Be sure to eat. I am off tomorrow, but I will see you on Thursday. *Au revoir*, Dorian."

Dorian was miserable and lonely that Wednesday, so he slept most of the day. That night he dreamed he was asleep in a nomadic tent. He heard a man say, "Sarah, prepare these strangers a meal." He went to the flap and looked out and saw three figures, all in robes, being entertained by an elderly man, also in a robe. He stared and suddenly one of the strangers caught his eye. It was Sophia. She smiled and looked down. And that was all. When he woke he longed for the visit of his new friend.

"Good morning Dorian, how did you sleep?" she seemed to sing her greeting to him.

"I had weird dreams."

"Can you tell me?"

"Maybe later. So, you promised to give me your verdict on Foucault."

"All in good time. I have something for you. Your own thermos. I will leave it with you and fill another each morning. That way you can enjoy a late afternoon cup of coffee at your leisure."

"Thank you, Sophia. Now pour me a cup will you, and share with me your thoughts of Foucault."

"Ah, Foucault. Dorian, can you imagine a human society that alone determines its thoughts, its actions, its destiny, apart from divine intervention?"

"How can it be otherwise?"

"*Voilà*, then all history is contingent. Listen to me. Foucault was a philosophical therapist seeking to free us from something he perceived as a kind of bondage. What mattered to him was the will to know and the pursuit of pleasure. But in his great attempt at bringing this conversation where it belonged for him, the stage of human experience, he was compromised, always compromised, because he never ceased to talk about the past, and the past was a past infatuated with a longing for God. And as much as he wished to move the conversation from talk about God to questions of oppression, tyranny, genocide, ironically his words liberated theologians from their own blindness.

"You see, Dorian, Foucault knew that theologians had for centuries dragged God into their own schemes of human liberation, and he set about to expose their utter failure. He saw how their designs led to a kind of widespread agnosis that exchanged the comfort of faith for shame. But you know he was doing his superb work on the heels of another extraordinary philosopher who influenced him and made incredible breakthroughs, Martin Heidegger. Heidegger chided philosophers to stop thinking about God."

"Bravo," Dorian chimed in. "But Heidegger was a Nazi. Doesn't that disqualify him in every sense of the word?"

"No, it is not so easy as that. You enter into a problematic practice of dismissing a body of thought for what? If we restrict judgment to moral intuitions we fail to judge the body of work on its merits. It is necessary to read through the oeuvre and make comparisons based on what is actually written. Rather we should explore why is it he said we should stop thinking about God, and ask whether the pronouncement is valid or meaningful. We have every right to consider Heidegger morally reprehensible, but we cannot be taken seriously unless we engage him critically."

Dorian thought he would cut to the chase. "Ah, but he was just following the trajectory of Nietzsche."

"Perhaps, but in either case, what might fill the vacuum left by this turn? May I suggest the void is being filled frivolously with replacement gods: happiness, prestige, wealth, pleasure. Tempting surrogates to fill the barren landscapes which are no more satisfying than the offerings of ancient sorcerers. Notice how recently the belief in magic has made an impressive recovery. It is contemporary history's trick of irony that when science alone can provide meaning the realm of magic will resurface. Scolded into believing that the numinous does not exist, people will flock to magic and cults, or they will worship at the altar of communication, imprisoned in a chaotic universe of contingency, confined to merely opportunistic relationships which work to their advantage."

Sophia continued, "What word do we have for blessing and curse without God in the mix? What word can stand against luck or chance unless it is destiny? What might be the deepest love without God? And as for meaning, Foucault exposed our late-modern penchant for criticizing everything to the point that our culture has been shattered and trust denied at all levels. We deconstruct our texts and evaluate them according to the truth game they play. But the relativism doesn't satisfy, and truth is stubborn and unwilling to be shortchanged."

"Too bad, Sophia, too bad." Dorian was unassuaged. "The chips have fallen where they may. We might wish for a Santa Claus, but wishing is all it is."

"Is that so? If we stop thinking about God, we stop being human."

"No, Sophia, beyond the accidents of our lives there is only the subject of the conversations. If there is any permanence to that, it is that it exists. The I of being beyond the accidents. That single *essent* and the history of conversations. Nothing more."

"Ah, a reference to Heidegger. Well, if that is the case, then we have no reason to engage in authentic or meaningful conversation. The record or texts of our civilization is all there is. But what of the reader of those texts? Unless the reader is somehow considered on his or her way to completion, then all that humankind can boast of is a massive pile of stories and interactions with no purpose. Are you not concerned about the fate of the reader? Is there room in your heart for compassion for the reader?"

"My heart—I . . . I'm not sure what you mean. But may I change the subject? I'd like to know how you learned all this?"

"Well, I read. In fact, beyond work and taking care of Pascal, all I do is read. Oh, and I dabble a little in poetry. And when I read Foucault I sensed his frustration at the never-ending stream of criticism, literary and otherwise, which he felt was debilitating. While appearing to be a crucible of truth, such criticism is itself a kind of punishment and forced discipline. In the end, Foucault found the endless flow of deconstruction circular and tending towards an infinite regress."

Dorian needed to back up. "But you said he knew that theologians had for centuries dragged God into their own schemes of human liberation, and he set about to expose their utter failure."

"Indeed, Foucault with the benefit of many of his excellent teachers recognized a fatal flaw in the Enlightenment's agenda.

With its commendable search for rationality in the pursuit of knowledge and truth, it floundered in its overestimation of the authority of reason. The period around the time of Immanuel Kant was especially exciting. The sense was that reason had self-evident first principles. It had the power to determine the validity of all beliefs. It could verify the soundness of moral convictions and religious claims. By virtue of its universality, it could explain everything in nature. It was as if by reason alone the world would become clear to us. But we misjudged reality's transparency. The hubris was considerable and led to the dangerous and chaotic thinking of Nietzsche. In fact, the world is massively complex, and the information we might gain is manifold. Philosophers began to argue that in order to make sense of it all and in order to thrive in it, human beings needed to acknowledge what they called their 'perspectives.' Honest recognition of those perspectives revealed that we are selective beings. Some of our various perspectives are accepted and others rejected, all without real grounding in any kind of ultimate truth. But this was the actual nature of knowing. It led to the theory that from our perspectives we integrate less complex cognitive models in order to orient ourselves and guide us in our behavior. Depending on the individual, some models are partial and specific, while others are meant for including us in perspectives common to a larger group of people and communities. These modes of life create a network of interdependent beliefs and practices. The philosophers of this school sought to address the self-defeating skepticism over reason's limits that produced an amorphous pluralism and relativism where, as Noel Coward insightfully sang, 'Anything Goes.' The goal was to allow for options and argumentation at every level such that thinking and choosing were free, but also recognized as a lifelong process of exchanging sounder beliefs and practices for the unsound ones. And as for language, the important breakthrough was to recognize the central role of signification, the way we convey meaning by signs or other symbolic means. We communicate with signs. Still, those behind this approach wanted to avoid collapsing into solipsism. The conclusion was that although we are the source of communication, that we create the signs that make language communication, we do not create the natural phenomena that also make up our world. That remains the world of our curiosity, our investigation. That belongs to nature. So, while culture can only exist because of our actions, nature exists independently of that. Certainly, cultural phenomena and natural phenomena exist together. Still, neither one can be reduced to or replaced by the other. There is an essential duality that can be seen in the use of both in order to derive from nature what is actually possible for cultural activity. But also, what is *good* for culture. The general consensus was that we are free agents but finite as well because we are by necessity bodily agents. We are always seeking ways of expanding our interests and bringing nature into the service of culture. But the lessening of our dependence on nature led to greater complexity in the moral and social spheres. The intractable duality of dependence and creativity revealed to a great extent the cultural relativism that makes moral behavior problematic."

Sophia took a deep breath and paused. "Dorian, I realize this is very deep, and I hope I'm not confusing you. May I just summarize?"

"Please do."

"The effect of the late modern and postmodern reaction to the Enlightenment was the conclusion by many that what was needed was not truth as the identity between what is observed in nature and the conclusions of the observer. Rather, it was translatability. The ability to establish mutual understanding. To creatively design a semiotic means useful for interpretation from both the perspective of free creativity and limited control."

Dorian was mollified. "I think I understand. Can you say where a favorite of mine, Richard Rorty, fits in with all this? You know he died not so long ago."

Sophia knew that Rorty had passed in 2007, ten years before. "Yes, I know. But I must go now, it's past time I should be on my rounds. Tomorrow I want to read something to you for your opinion, and then I will answer your question about Rorty. *Au revoir.*"

Sophia arrived the next morning at her usual time and in her usual good humor. She didn't bother with hellos and simply embarked on another crazy story about Pascal. "Dorian you won't believe this. I was on the computer last night working on a poem called 'When Cats Sing Birdsongs' when Pascal jumped up on my desk and looked straight at me. I mean he literally stared without blinking once, and then he pushed and held down the backspace key. It was soooo crazy! He held it just long enough to erase everything I had written. It was as if he hated the poem and knew I hadn't backed anything up." And then she let out a great animated laugh that tossed her hair up and around her shoulders. Dorian couldn't suppress a smile.

Calmed but still grinning from ear to ear, Sophia said, "Anyway, yesterday you mentioned your heart and I felt as though it was unknown to you, and I remembered a favorite poet of mine, W. H. Auden, and his poem 'To You Simply.'"

"I didn't mention my heart."

"Yes you did, you said 'my heart.'"

"But only because you brought it up."

"Either way, I thought of Auden, and here it is."

Dorian had no opportunity to protest as Sophia once again launched herself onto his bed.

> For what as easy
> For what though small,
> For what is well
> Because between,
> To you simply
> From me I mean
> Who goes with who
> The bedclothes say,
> As I and you
> Go kissed away,
> The data given,
> The senses even
> Fate is not late,
> Nor the speech rewritten,
> Nor one word forgotten,

Said at the start
About heart,
By heart, for heart.

Again, there was an eerie silence as the room closed in on Dorian, and there was only space for the two of them. No bed, no table and chairs, nothing but the two of them. Dorian breached the stillness. "Sophia, why read that poem to me?"

"Because of your heart."

"You assume I have one." Before Sophia could object he silenced her with his fake laugh. This time he himself heard how hollow it sounded. He frowned and pushed his agenda. "You promised you would speak to me of Rorty."

Sophia eyed him suspiciously, then appeased him. "Indeed, it is essentially where we left off before. Foucault, benefiting from his many brilliant teachers, recognized a fatal flaw in the Enlightenment's agenda. With its commendable search for rationality in the pursuit of knowledge and truth, it stumbled in its overestimation of the authority of reason. Rorty perhaps better than anyone in America exposed that failure to a larger reading public. But Rorty couldn't have grown up the way he did and remained an analytical philosopher. Instead, his parents' activism was the catalyst for his later empathetic pragmatism. Although he could not completely jettison his analytical past, he was essentially a pragmatist in the tradition of Dewey. That is to say, Rorty believed the best hope for philosophy was not to practice philosophy. His most serious caveat on pragmatism was that it needed to eschew its scientistic characteristics and focus on its connection to Romanticism."

Sophia continued, "But there is a kind of strange twist to the story of Richard Rorty. When I read a late interview with him shortly before his death I found something quite interesting. The interviewer appeared to be a believer in God, and yet he was a big fan of Rorty. He was trying to get him to open up to the possibility of transcendence. Rorty was not having it, but then in a strange moment of what—doubt, doubt about his own beliefs?—he said 'maybe.' I can't get that out of my head."

Dorian felt defensive. "Perhaps he succumbed to the fear of his own mortality?"

"I don't know, but I doubt it. He may have simply been following his own logic. Rorty wasn't so much an atheist as an agnostic. He was very good at being clear about the validity of philosophical claims. But he wasn't given over to expounding on ultimate reality, except perhaps to say there is no ultimate reality. Isn't it interesting that his turn toward pragmatism included an outpouring of empathy for the marginalized, the disempowered, the economically oppressed, and on it went? But his style was that of a provocateur much like Socrates. A question asker. Still, his work led to new kinds of thinking, thinking especially regarding the role of relationships in the pursuit of philosophical honesty. It led to a whole body of work being done on the role of recognition."

Sophia continued to provide background. "The turn actually began with Hegel, who was perhaps the first to explore human freedom and liberty in terms of recognition. Hegel surmised that true freedom is itself a mutual act of recognition between people such that each can recognize himself or herself in the other. Fichte put it this way: we must treat each other as free in order to ourselves be truly free. I find this breakthrough exciting because it seems to me that the human soul cannot thrive without recognition. Human worth and our sense of reality are not something prior to social interaction. It is the result of being recognized in our social context. Any hope of a just world demands that we all recognize each other."

"What is just about the world?" Dorian remained cynical.

"But that's the point Dorian," Sophia pleaded. "The world is not just, but that is no reason not to insist that it must be just: to work for justice, to find ways of allowing for the flourishing of all human beings. There have been recent breakthroughs in this, and Rorty was an avatar for the disenfranchised. The more recent breakthrough has to do with overcoming philosophy's fixation with communication and moving forward with an inquiry into recognition. Much of this is the result of a great deal of research into human psychology, sociology, but also biology; appreciation of the inseparability of mind and body. The research simply asked, allowing for the necessity of recognition, how does it happen, and how do we know that a person has recognized another? The results showed that it can only happen when as children we learn to balance self-possession and the necessary feeling of independence with identification with others. Failing in that, it just may be that a person becomes incapable of love."

Dorian was alarmed. "Wait. Something happens to some people, what when they are prevented from recognizing their freedom *in* others? And so, they cannot love? Preposterous."

"No, Dorian, it is the result of a large body of scientific evidence. And I saw it so clearly lived out on a macro level in France. Perhaps beginning with the great thinker Rousseau, it became popular to so highly prize our individual freedom that we became blind to the limits of our bloody, hard-fought-for liberalism. Rousseau fretted that when we are constrained by the opinions of others, we lose our freedom, we lose ourselves.

"That would be my view, Sophia."

"Dorian, say it isn't so, because Rousseau did not realize that we cannot be ourselves unless we recognize others. It was the same with Sartre. He was terrified by the loss of his 'self' in his encounter with the 'other,' and his work influenced a whole nation, no all of Western culture, to the point that we in France often fail to recognize the importance of intersubjectivity. A necessary balance has been lost. I see it here too in America. But what is emerging is a kind of pushback. The linguistic and cultural focus has recently come under fire once again and for good reason. Dorian, do you know anything about queer theory?"

"Yes, I encountered it a few years back, and I found it credible."

"Good, so do I. It corresponds with affect theory. So much previous work was done in the kind of wary confidence you can recognize in Rorty and several others, that the focus on texts, language, and in various and complicated ways discourse within a humanistic trajectory, might lead to effecting positive change. But what remained was still too much attention to language as the key to understanding humankind. Granted, language is the source of accurate communication, and it may even be a way by which we come to the truth, however that might be construed. But language is also the means by which we lie, it is the way we bully and intimidate others, the way we seduce the gullible. As quickly as a classic piece of literature appears so does a spate of child pornography, an internet page filled with hateful stereotypes and blatant falsehoods. In the end, the latest language models appear as no more than images of ourselves as prejudiced, sexist, naive, personable, kind, loving, and doting. Which just might be a reflection of the models themselves."

Sophia went on, "In light of this the discussion turned to translatability as the rational way to move toward human flourishing; the idea of exchanging bad ideas and behavior for preferable ones, not because of a discovery of identity, but within the context of translatability. What this fresh body of research focused on was the ways in which human behavior in such social settings as religion, politics, economics, etc., are shaped by influences other than discursive practices. Rather, this research focused on desire, emotion, and feeling."

Dorian was recalling his introduction to QT. "Yes, I found it all quite liberating. The upshot, as I recall, was that our actions cannot be explained simply by semiotic experience, and that our behavior is essentially mysterious and beyond our control. So, we should simply follow our desires. I fully support that idea."

"Sorry, I think that is a weak conclusion and not particularly helpful in the long run, and this is why. You're missing the nuance of QT and its recognition of the tension within us. Yes, we may follow our deepest desires, but we don't always want to, and sometimes we resist those compulsions. Also, yes QT essentially rejected the Enlightenment theory of humans as rational subjects complete with our own autonomy, and that we are sovereign over our personal emotions. Moreover, it put into question the idea that cultivating virtues by habit, something the ancient theologians called habituation, would lead to virtuous people. These traditional ideas fell far short of understanding what humans really feel and do. Desire appeared to the researchers far more inscrutable than previously thought. Hence the moniker 'queer,' for the strangeness of desire. This was in part a negative reaction to previous conclusions that physiological arousal, the upwelling of desire, was utterly malleable and acted within the confines of our mental faculties. That our feelings and desires arise from discursive social construction. The problem uncovered by the researchers was that the previous theory did not recognize behaviors that acted outside of that theory, which meant that an entire realm of thought and behavior was being ignored. The old theory entirely missed a whole range of inelastic and non-fixed areas of experience and knowledge. The term 'affect' was applied to represent the way that, for example, Foucault's kind of formations of power relationships are neither universal to human beings as in the old model, nor are they simply artifacts found in the archeology of discursive construction. They are in many ways mysterious, deeply emotional, and arise from within us. The simple fact is that people often do the opposite of what they want or believe."

Dorian was trying to work through all this. "But how is that different from what I just concluded?"

"I will get to that, but first let me say what the research points to. First, individuals do not have sovereignty over their decisions, over their will. This was a clinical breakthrough of momentous importance. We cannot always do or act in a way that we might want. No matter how hard we try, we will desire certain things and we will often pursue those desires regardless of the consequences. Regardless of what we have been instructed to believe and do. Even beyond what we ourselves might think we should do."

Dorian was confused. "But that was my very point."

"Yes, but there is more to it. While affect theory did reject the old idea that meaning and experience are fundamentally cultural constructs produced in discursive practice, it did not minimize the importance of language. Linguistic analysis remained an important tool. However, reason and language are here recognized as merely two of the many things that make people act in certain ways. In fact, the way reason and language attach to affects largely determines both the character of our reasoning and the language we use. But what must always be kept in mind is that this research was not meant to condone, condemn, or excuse behavior, but rather it was meant to offer insights into the mystery of human behavior."

"Right but given that, I'm free to draw my own conclusions." Dorian still hadn't captured the nuance.

"No, that's the point. You may *not* be able to draw conclusions that conflict with your affections. So, we can't get there from here. Rather, we have to sort out what the research might mean and of course, it will mean different things to different people. I personally want to think of this in terms of ethics because it could certainly lead to a more tolerant view of human fallibility. But on the other hand, behaviorally speaking, we are just as inclined to judge people as we are to tolerate them. Bigotry may not be so easily overcome by rational means. But equally, egalitarianism may be found in individuals without any rational explanation. The theologian Paul of Tarsus wrote that 'what I want to do, I do not do, but what I hate I do.' This seems to me to throw light on the paradox, and it turns on Paul's point. Especially when he says 'I have the desire to do what is good . . .'"

Sophia continued, "For me, it all revolves around seeing the other in ourselves. It is the speculative insight that to be capable of love is to see ourselves in others. That is the only way to self-love, the opposite being a steady decline into lovelessness and self-loathing. But if the virtues are essential for the process of inner recognition and freedom, and we have very little power to change our deep desires, what hope might there be for a more just and peaceful world? What hope might there be that I myself will ever be able to do what I want to do? The answer I believe, is that we have access to a source that can produce alternative desires in us if we are open to it. That we might possibly replace unwelcome desires with the desires we want. I guess what I'm saying is that human salvation comes not from within us but from outside us."

"Where are you going with this?" Dorian was pretty sure he disagreed.

"Perhaps it is time you perceived things in a new way."

"I can't change."

"No, never, never give up what you know to be true, and never think you can or should be someone you're not. It's impossible anyway. Rather, merely to perceive things in a new way.

"Oh, my, look at the time. Dorian, I have to get about my rounds, but I have something to read to you tomorrow that will perhaps open up some new possibilities."

"So, you will read to me tomorrow, and *voilà*, all this will become clear?" This time Dorian's laugh burst out from deep inside him and was truly authentic.

"We will see, *au revoir*." She blew him a kiss and Dorian reeled.

He slept peacefully that night without dreams, a rarity for him these days. Although his inclination was to reject everything Sophia was saying, her confidence but also her genuineness, had placated him. When she arrived with his breakfast the next morning he was eager for her company. His symptoms had stabilized but had not vanished. He still had terrible bouts of nausea and bloating, and he had trouble keeping his food down. His weight had dwindled to a hundred and twenty pounds, and he had lost all the muscle mass he had spent years developing. But he was most despondent over his hair which was coming out in clumps. At this rate, he knew he would soon be bald. But all that seemed to fade as Sophia put down the breakfast tray and poured the coffee from Dorian's new thermos. He ate what he could and then turned to her and said, "Please read to me what you promised."

Sophia became pensive and said, "I have never read one of my poems to anyone before. Well, other than Pascal." In her hand was a leaf of parchment paper embellished by an accomplished hand at calligraphy. "I'm not sure they are very good, and I feel embarrassed. But this one contains the message I wanted to convey yesterday, and I think it does it better than my feeble philosophy ever could. May I read it to you? It's quite short."

"Of course, please."

"It is called 'To W. H. Auden in Reflection on His Conversion.'"

Are we who bles'd
  by Wholly Other life
who cannot breach
  the infinite chasm
nor hope to
  made no more real
  by weak signs
feeble figures, mirrors, and stage
here brought to understand
rent curtain
  this all-conquering death
  among the bones
the God-shattered ruins
comes forth life
  Also wakened?
Neath proscenium arch
no longer dead
a now perfected work
not of us

"Hmmm. Well, I'm not sure I have any real sense of what you are saying."

"That's all right," Sophia consoled. "I will leave it with you if you don't mind."

"Fine. Listen, Sophia, what are you doing Sunday? You know, I never see you on Sundays. But this Sunday I heard they are having a Tom Jones impersonator here followed by a barbecue. I wondered if you would join me?"

"Yes, I know, but the reason you never see me on Sunday is that I go to Mass. It's something I never miss and am committed to."

"All day?"

"After Mass, I'm a eucharistic minister at local hospitals."

"Can you make an exception? I'd really like to have you there with me."

"Sorry, Dorian, this is something very sacred to me, and I would be loath to miss it."

"Sure, I understand." The reply was totally out of Dorian's character, and yet he meant it.

"How about another cup of coffee?" Dorian nodded and Sophia poured. They chatted for a short while about nothing much of importance, and then Sophia was off to do her rounds. She was off that Saturday, and when Sunday came around Dorian was feeling morose and considered not going to the concert and barbecue. However, the staff nurse insisted, and Dorian was too anxious and distraught to put up a fight.

The room was filled with the elderly bathed and renewed in a musical fountain of youth. Heads were bobbing to the sound of a realistic-looking and sounding impersonator. When he belted out the lyrics to "What's New Pussycat?" it brought the enthusiastic residents to their feet, up and dancing in makeshift aisles, at least the ones that could stand. But even the wheelchairs were swaying back and forth. Dorian was content to sit still and listen, his nurse by his side. Naturally, the whole thing inspired a sing-along, and so unbeknownst to the jubilant band the air was compromised. Always unseen, a deadly microbe once again threatened humanity. None the wiser, more than their joy was contagious, and then Dorian looked at the door and in walked Sophia. She strode over to a nearby empty chair and scooted it next to his wheelchair. She sat down and put her hand on his and they listened together. After thirty minutes she whispered in his ear that she needed to go. She thanked him for inviting her. He said he was so happy she could come, and then she was gone.

She was off again on Monday and Dorian counted the hours until Tuesday morning when she appeared in her regular jovial manner. Ignoring the breakfast tray, he asked her to sit near him on the bed and she complied. "Sophia, I need to tell you something. Something really, really important. Sophia, I love you!"

Sophia's glistening white smile broke open wide and she said, "I love you too, Dorian."

"No, Sophia, I don't mean it like that. Hell, you love everybody. I mean like in love, real love. The kind that means being together forever. Husband and wife kind of love."

"So do I, Dorian."

"How can you say that? Look at me. Can't you see I'm useless to you? You're so much younger than I, and, and I'm falling apart. My head is going bald, my body is shriveling up. I'm wasting away."

"*L'amour ne se soucie pass de l'âge.*"

"Sophia, you know I don't speak French."

"I think you are very special Dorian, and I don't care how old you are."

Dorian was astounded, so much so that he couldn't speak. She spoke instead. "Have you thought about the future, Dorian?"

"I have none, and that's another reason you should have nothing to do with me."

Sophia waved a dismissive hand. "No matter, I have something to read to you if you will let me."

"I will always want to hear you read."

"This one is by T. S. Eliot called 'Death by Water.'"

Phlebas the Phoenician, a fortnight dead,
Forgot the cry of gulls, and the deep sea swell
And the profit and loss.
A current under sea
Picked his bones in whispers. As he rose and fell
He passed the stages of his age and youth
Entering the whirlpool.
Gentile or Jew
O you who turn the wheel and look to windward,
Consider Phlebas, who was once handsome and tall as you.

Silence. It was Dorian who spoke first. "Again, your choice of poems perplexes me. Why won't you tell me what you're getting at?"

"Dorian, are you baptized?"

"Yes, but what does it matter? I have never practiced in any serious manner."

"No matter. I confess I read this poem more for me than for you. But it pleases me, and it makes sense to me, and it will bring you comfort if you let it. I will script a copy and give it to you on Thursday. *La mort par l'eau est la vie par l'eau.*"

"I told you I don't speak French."

"I know. Listen I must be on my way. I'm off again for two days but I will see you Thursday."

"Sophia, I think I know where you are going with this, and I would do anything to please you. But this whole God thing is beyond mysterious to me. I might look from now until eternity, and yet I am sure I will neither find God nor will I find any evidence of his existence. After all, it was one of your favorites, Augustine I believe, who said, 'How shall I find God, if I have no memory of you?'"

Sophia whispered, "Never mind, he will find you."

"Wait, before you go I want you to have this. It's a sealed envelope to be opened by you alone if something should happen to me. I've made you executor and sole heir to my estate."

Sophia was taken aback. "Dorian, that's not necessary."

"Oh yes, it is. Otherwise, everything I have worked for all my life will be pillaged by lawyers and the state of New York. Please, just take the envelope. It will help me sleep at night."

"If you insist. Now get some rest."

Late Tuesday night Dorian woke feeling awful as if he had terrible flu. He was back and forth to the bathroom all night nearly crawling. The staff was oblivious. They seemed overwhelmed. Something had gone terribly wrong in the nursing home. Not until early morning when Dorian was having trouble breathing did they become attentive. He overheard the nurse say, "I hope it's not another case of COVID."

It was indeed, and on Wednesday, February 29, 2020, Dorian Fist was admitted to Jackson Memorial Hospital where he was immediately rushed to ICU. The floor was crowded and every bed taken, each one a victim of the COVID-19 pandemic which was ravaging Florida nursing homes. It would spread like wildfire to bars, homes, and hospitals, but its most deadly landing was in nursing facilities. It fell like the plague it was. When Sophia arrived for work on Thursday she learned of Dorian's fate. She finished her shift and drove to Jackson Memorial. No one was allowed in ICU, so she sat with a mask and gloves in the adjacent waiting room. When she asked the nurse how serious his condition was, the nurse replied "grave." "He can no longer breathe on his own, and we're putting him on a ventilator." Sophia sat despondently in the waiting room for an hour and then went home. After work the following day she returned and once again was not allowed in ICU. No one was but the medical staff and support team. The pandemic was front-page news, and the international crisis of death, overcrowded hospitals, and decimated nursing homes were producing a sense of shock and helplessness throughout the world.

Sophia came again on Saturday and again after Mass on Sunday, passing on her usual communion visits. She sat silent, miserable that she could not at least be by his side. On Sunday, late afternoon, the nurse came out to her. "We did everything we could, but I'm afraid he's gone." Dorian Fist was sixty-eight years old.

Sophia said, "May I see him?"

"He's no longer breathing, so it's OK, but keep your mask and gloves on and don't touch anything, especially the patient. We're still not sure how this thing is spread."

Looking down at him she softly wept and then noticed her poem on Auden in his right hand. The nurse was standing at her side. "Are you his wife?"

"No."

"Next of kin?"

"No, just a friend."

"Then, you really shouldn't be here. Do you know whom we should call?" Sophia handed her a three by five card with a name, address, and telephone number. It read Leslie Ann Peters, 2508 Park Street, Pomona, CA, and it was listed with a phone number.

"That's his only surviving blood relative. It's his daughter, but they were estranged. I will let her know you will be calling. Can you give me a day? Is that OK?"

"Sure, we have to make arrangements with the coroner anyway, and he's completely overwhelmed."

That evening Sophia called the California number and Leslie Ann Peters picked up after the second ring. "Hi, this is Leslie."

"Hi. My name is Sophia Milhaud."

There was silence on the other end.

"Leslie, I know you don't know me, and this is going to come as a great shock to you, but I am a friend of your father."

"My what?"

"Your father. Of course, this seems impossible, but it is true. He has just passed away in Miami Beach. Listen, I felt it only right to contact you. As I understand it you are his only living blood relative, and with a simple DNA test that can be proven. I also wanted you to know because your father was a very wealthy man, and there are no claims to his estate. It's all yours if you want it. The hospital will call you tomorrow or at least very soon, soon as they can. It's up to you how you will respond. Again, I only thought it right to share this with you."

Again, a long silence, and then Leslie Ann haltingly replied, "This is so hard. I'm sorry, what was your name again?"

"Sophia, Sophia Milhaud."

"Sophia, this is so hard to fathom. I, I don't know what to say."

"Leslie, please just think about it, you have some time. Is your mother still living?"

"Yes, she's just across the street."

"Well, the two of you and your loved ones will never have to worry over finances again if you so choose. It's all there is for him now."

"Did he wish this?"

"I would love to say yes, but we never spoke of it."

"But then how did you know?"

"Les, I have to go. From now on the matter is in your hands, and God bless you. Goodbye."

"Goodbye, and thanks, I think." Leslie Ann held the now silent cell phone in her shaking hand for some time and then touched the red icon to an already dead signal. It suddenly occurred to her that only her father called her Les. It was something she never spoke of—something she never shared with anybody other than her mother.

In spite of the danger on Monday morning, Sophia returned to her duties at Ravenswood. Precautions were ramped up, but patients were dying in unprecedented numbers. In what was later recognized as a monumental blunder, COVID patients were being moved from inundated hospitals to nursing homes, in effect creating virus incubators. Still, the patients had to be fed and looked after. She knocked on the open door of Eleanor Welsh. The charming accent rang out again song-like. "I have your breakfast, Eleanor. I heard you had an especially bad night. Perhaps I can read to you. It might make you feel better?"